WHERE
DARKNESS LIES

OTHER TITLES BY BELLA JEWEL

WHERE
DARKNESS LIES

Bella Jewel

Montlake
Romance

Text copyright © 2014 Bella Jewel

Published by Montlake Romance, Seattle

www.apub.com

Amazon, the Amazon logo, and Montlake Romance are trademarks of Amazon.com, Inc., or its affiliates.

ISBN-13: 9781612184920
ISBN-10: 1612184928

Cover design by bürosüd° München, www.buerosued.de

Library of Congress Control Number: 2014912204

Printed in the United States of America

To my husband, my biker, my always and forever.

PROLOGUE

Dimitri

Revenge is a dish best served cold.

That's the way I am serving it—cold, empty, broken, and completely fucked up.

The need for revenge is all consuming. Did I ever plan to spend ten years of my life searching for a man just to seek retribution? No. But it's all I am now. It's all I know. It's all I breathe. My life spiraled down into darkness a long time ago, and darkness became all I knew. It's all I know now.

You can't save someone from themselves—not when they don't want to be saved.

Once darkness reaches in and takes hold of your heart, there's no going back. It takes your life and it steers it on paths you never wanted or planned. But you go with it, because darkness has the control now. I have accepted what I am. I have accepted that my path has been chosen. I have accepted that I will do whatever it takes to make him pay.

I *am* where darkness lies.

CHAPTER ONE

Jess

The ship sways, jerking me from the void that has been surrounding me on and off for the past two days. I lick my lower
lip, tasting the dry, coppery blood there. My head aches, I've gone
beyond hungry now. I'm just desperate for something, anything.
Hell, a glass of water wouldn't hurt. I try to blink but my eyes are so
dry they burn. I move my aching, distressed body and try to focus
on the room around me.

I'm still in the cell.

And he still hasn't come back.

I know who has me. I heard his name—*Dimitri*. Hendrix's
stepson. I know this, because I have been on Hendrix's ship since he
saved me all those years ago, and have, plenty of times, overheard
conversations about his damaged stepson whom he abandoned at
the age of fifteen. I guess Dimitri wasn't going to just sit back and
move on with his life.

I close my eyes, taking a deep breath.

I can survive this. It's a revenge tactic, which means he won't kill
me . . . not yet, anyway. He wants Hendrix, he wants a fight, and so
he will keep me alive. He might not take care of me, but he'll keep
me here until he gets what he wants. I slowly push to my feet, and

the chains around my ankles rattle. Where do they think I'm going to go on a ship? Dive overboard and kill myself? Maybe attack them with a piece of rotting wood? Seriously. Dimitri clearly has no idea how knowledgeable I am when it comes to the ocean.

Dimitri—the angel of darkness.

I think back to when I first looked at him. Somewhat like an angel all wrapped in black. To look at, he's absolutely breathtaking. The kind of breathtaking that not only steals your breath but causes your entire body to stop working. His eyes are the color of baby blue blankets and his skin is that creamy olive that only so many people can pull off when they have such fair eyes. His hair is thick, whipping around his shoulders. It's dark. Like him. I will never understand how such beauty can be the home of such darkness.

I shuffle over to the door but my chains clank just before I reach it; I'm in a wooden room with no windows and no spaces to see through. The only gap is a small hole in the door that's far too high for me to see anything. With my tiny frame, there's no way I could ever get elevated enough. I manage to shuffle around the cell as much as my chains will allow, shoving at the walls I can reach in a pathetic attempt to find a weakness in them. I know better, though. I've been on a ship for long enough to know how sturdy they are.

My body is so damned sore, like I'm living with a bad cold each day. It's probably because last night, in my haze, I froze. It was so cold, and I had no blanket to cover me up. I shivered and groaned, rolling for most of the night. The least they could do is give me a blanket, but apparently luxuries such as that aren't in the deal. Sniffling, I find my spot back on the floor and sit down.

Hendrix will find me.

I know he will.

He's been my protector since that awful night all those years ago. He made promises to me, and I know he'll keep them. I know he'll come after me, but what scares me the most is the damage that might come to him in doing so. Dimitri—he's the essence of gloom. His kind of damaged runs deep. I honestly don't know what kind of danger I'm in, or what kind of danger I'm putting Hendrix in.

I just know this situation isn't good.

I have to hang in there, though. I've lived through worse. These kinds of things, they don't scare me the way they scare most people. I've run with the ultimate criminals and I've seen things most wouldn't see in their lifetime. What most people *shouldn't* see in their lifetime. I'm prepared for whatever is thrown at me. I'll keep my cool. I won't show fear, and I won't let him see any kind of weakness in me.

I won't break.

It's just not who I am.

~

My chin is pressed against my chest and I'm exhausted by the time he shows his face again. I've only seen him once since I've been here, and it was when he threw me down into this cell, slamming my body against the cold wooden wall. That's when I split my lip. He didn't speak, he didn't even look at me, he just tossed me down and left. I was starting to wonder if he'd show up again, or if he'd just leave me down here to die.

I lift my head when I hear his boots stomping on the wooden floor. The door rattles and a moment later, it's swung open and he comes in. I stare at him, in complete awe. It's hard not to when someone is as beautiful as he is. His dark hair hangs heavy around his face and his expression is hard. His eyes, though beautiful, hold a whole lot of pain. He's wearing a hoodie that covers his large torso, and his jeans are met with heavy black boots. The ultimate bad boy. In every way.

"Get up," he growls, his voice rugged and rough.

I do as he asks. There is no point in arguing. I need to be sassy and strong, to make sure that he doesn't break me, but at the same time I'm not making him angrier. At least, I'd like to think that's the case. As soon as I am on my feet, his hand lashes out and grips my arm. His fingers bite into my skin and I smother my wince.

"Where are you taking me?" I ask in a small, scratchy voice. It's the first time I've heard my voice in days.

"None of your business."

Damned pirates. They give nothing away.

"Is this your ship?" I push as he undoes my chains and tugs me toward the door.

"Don't fuckin' insult me."

Insult him? Why would that insult him? I shuffle my feet as best I can as he pulls me out of the door. His tugging becomes more persistent, and the frustration at trying to keep up becomes overwhelming. When I stumble and struggle to catch my footing for the fourth time, I finally snap.

"Stop tugging me so hard, pirate," I growl under my breath.

Before I can say another word, he has spun around, gripped my shoulders, and slammed me up against the nearest wall. When he's up close like this, I can see the jagged scar to the left of his lip. I can also see how stunning his eyes truly are. They're not just blue, they have little speckles of aqua through them, giving them that unique color all their own. I squirm as his fingers dig into my shoulders, but I keep my face emotionless.

"You ever insult me like that again, I'll make it hurt . . ." he growls, shaking me a little.

"How did I insult you?" I gasp, squirming again.

"I might be a lot of things, but I'm not a fuckin' pirate, and if I so much as hear that word leave your lips again, I'll make you wish it didn't. I'm not scum, not like that piece of shit pirate I took you from."

4

"Funny that," I growl. "Because you're the one who stole and starved an innocent girl."

He leans in close, letting his eyes burn into mine. "There ain't no innocence in anything that comes from hell, girl."

He thinks I'm a pirate, and for some reason I don't want to correct him. Maybe it's a good thing he thinks he's gotten something that is important to Hendrix. If I tell him I'm just a stray, who really, in the big scheme of things, isn't that important, then he'll likely kill me. If I need to play along for now, so be it. I don't correct him.

Instead I narrow my eyes. "What are you expecting to get out of this?"

He smiles, and it's cold and empty. "One word: revenge."

CHAPTER TWO

Jess

I have to blink, at least four times. I can't be seeing this right. We're . . . we're . . . on land. At a wharf, with a lineup of SUVs waiting for us. I felt the ship rocking a few times, but I didn't think it was because we were coming in to land. I thought Dimitri was a pirate, I thought this battle would happen on the ocean, but I've just learned how very wrong I was. My heart seizes. How is Hendrix supposed to know I'm on land? How is he supposed to find me here? I let my eyes dart around, trying to take in my surroundings.

We're in America somewhere, that much I know. The scenery is very familiar and the SUV license plates indicate so. I'm too far away to see which state is stamped on them. My legs wobble as Dimitri pulls me down the ramps and leads me directly to the large vehicles. He opens the door of one and shoves me inside. I land on my face, hands tangled beneath me. I squeak and try to roll, but it's not easy when you can't use your own hands to push yourself up. Mine are handcuffed and moving is next to impossible without them.

I manage to shove myself up to my knees just as Dimitri gets into the front seat of the SUV. Two large men join us. One, who is bald and absolutely huge, gets in the front seat, lifting a gun and placing it on his lap. A silent threat. The other is darker-skinned, and has a more gentle face. He climbs in the back beside me when I finally get myself onto my bottom.

The SUV surges forward and I find my breath hitching. I won't lie and say fear isn't washing through me right now, because it is. When we were on the water, it was easy enough to hope and assume that Hendrix would find me. He knows the ocean. The land, however, it's . . . it's a lot harder. What if he doesn't even know I'm here? Miles and miles of ocean he could be wasting his time on.

I swallow and close my eyes, calming myself. The good thing about land is that I have more chance of escape. That's a plus. I can escape out here if given the right moment. I will hope for that moment, because it might be the only chance. *I* might be my only chance. I open my eyes and peer out of the window. Tall trees, wide roads, and people on bicycles whizz past. A strange feeling swells in my chest, and it takes me a moment to recognize it.

I'm on land again.

It's been over two years since I've been in civilization, and it's quite an overwhelming feeling. People chatter, cars pass by noisily. My head feels clogged. I'm so used to nothing but the sound of crashing waves that I wonder how I ever felt at peace in this place. On water is the only place I have ever felt serene. Tranquil.

I turn and stare at the front of the car to catch Dimitri watching me in the rearview mirror. I narrow my eyes and glare at him. He returns the glare and turns his eyes back to the road. "Where are you taking me?" I ask, tugging on my chains.

"I'm not tellin' you where we're goin', nor am I going to discuss anything with you. You speak when I tell you to. Until such time, you keep your mouth shut and do as you're told."

"That's fine by me—I've run with assholes long enough to know how people like you work," I quip. "If you think I'm telling you anything about Hendrix, you're very wrong. If you want me to shut up, then I will shut up."

Dimitri slams on the breaks and I go surging forward. It's then I realize I'm not wearing a seatbelt. My face smashes against the back of his chair and my nose cracks. Blood pours down my face. I wail loudly and reach up, feeling my fingers become coated in the warm, sticky liquid. I hear Dimitri's door slam, and then mine is pulled open. He grips me by my shoulders and hurls me out of the car.

"Here's the thing, girl," he snarls, pulling me close. I'm sure any other time I'd be able to smell him, he's that close, but all I can smell is my own blood as it fills my nose. "You don't get a say in how this goes down. You don't answer my questions, you will find yourself six feet under. Get my drift? I'll leave it up to you to decide how much your life is worth. Stop protecting that no good son of a bitch. He deserves to fuckin' die a long, painful death."

"You don't know him," I say in a small, angry voice. "You know only what you have created in your head, but it's so far from the—"

"Shut up!" he bellows. "Don't tell me what I know and what I don't know. You haven't lived my life so don't go tellin' me what I've created."

"You're wasting your time," I whisper. "He's not going to give in to you."

His eyes flicker. "He'll do whatever I fuckin' want, because I saw how he looked at you. If you were worth nothing, girl, then he would have shot me down and risked your life. He didn't. Now, get back in that car and shut your mouth."

My hands tremble with emotion, and I turn and shuffle back into the car. There are so many words I want to say, but what good will they do? He's sticking with whatever crazy story he's created about Hendrix in his head, and he's not backing down. I don't expect him to, but I have to do whatever I can to protect myself. This man, he's on the edge. I don't know how far I can push him, because I can't read him.

All I see is hatred.

A hatred so deep I wonder what else is in there.

We pull up at a massive house. It's surrounded by a solid, black iron fence that's easily eight feet high. I shiver. That's not going to be easy to escape from. Inside that fence is a huge three-story home. It's made of sandstone and is quite stunning. The boundary of the property boasts thick trees and bushes, clearly for privacy. When the car comes to a stop at the front door, I stare out. *Wow.*

Dimitri gets out of the SUV and comes straight to my door. He opens it, takes my arm, and pulls me out. He tugs me toward the front door and the two large men follow. I trip on the steps with these stupid chains on my feet, and with a growl he leans down and unlocks them. "Try to escape," he hisses. "I'll cut your fuckin' feet off."

"Because that's a logical threat," I mutter.

He stares at me for a minute, in shock or rage, I don't know. His face is blank.

He swings the front door of the house open, and we step inside. I lose my breath. The house is massive. All polished wooden floors, maroon rugs, dark furniture. There is extravagant artwork hanging on the walls, the kind of art that's twisted. Dark figures curled around strange things, or women, looking broken, naked, and damaged. I shiver.

Dimitri leads me down the hall, and we pass numerous large rooms, including a white wood kitchen to die for and a ballroom. Jesus, this house has a little of everything. I imagine I'll be spending my time in a cell, but in a place like this, it's probably luxury. I try to take in as much as I can as I'm tugged down the halls. Dimitri walks with determination, his large body quite overwhelming from this angle. He's so much bigger than me.

He takes me up a flight of stairs, and I notice that the two guards are behind us still. We get to the top of the stairs and he swings tightly to the left, gripping a door handle and shoving it open. We step into a massive room. I gape—it's nearly bigger than Hendrix's entire ship. I don't hesitate when Dimitri shoves me in; instead, my eyes widen with shock.

Thick, soft carpet, a big white bed, a bathroom with a spa, a massive lounge and television, and that's just the basics. It's outfitted with only the nicest spreads, curtains, and rugs. Dimitri obviously has a shitload of money—that or this isn't his house. I get the feeling it is, though. I turn with big, deer-in-headlight eyes, and meet Dimitri's angry glare.

"You'll stay in here. The door locks, you can't get out. You'll have everything you need, and I'll use you as I see fit."

Use me?

He obviously sees the confusion on my face.

"Don't flatter yourself, girl. I mean I will use you to piece together my plan. You'll give me information. You will accompany me anyplace I need to go, because I don't trust anyone but myself. I won't have you escaping."

Great.

I place my hands on my hips. "I have nowhere to escape to. In case you didn't notice, I lived on a ship. Maybe you never questioned it, but there's usually a reason a girl like me is on a ship away from land."

He narrows his eyes. "Girls like you are on those ships for one reason and one reason only; we both know what that is."

Oh.

He.

Did.

Not.

"I beg your pardon?" I whisper, feeling my hands shaking.

"Pirates like Hendrix don't keep women on their ships. There's only one purpose for them, and that's to fuck."

I feel my body begin to quake. He has no idea. No idea that I never, not once, fucked one person on Hendrix's ship. He has no idea that I have never willingly had sex. He has no idea that the idea of being called someone's whore is enough to break every strength I've built up inside me.

"You. Know. Nothing. About. Me," I bite out.

His eyes flare. "I know enough."

"You're so cocky, aren't you?" I snap. "So damned sure of yourself. You think you know how this is going to go down. You think you have picked the right person to make Hendrix come to you. If I'm just a whore, asshole, then what purpose would he have to come after me?"

His face tightens and he lashes out, curling his fingers around my shoulder. He hurls me close, lifting me off the ground so I'm dangling in front of him.

"I've had enough of your loud mouth. This is your last warning, girl. Shut it or I'll shut it for you."

I launch my knee up, hitting him right in the groin. It's a surprise attack, but it works. He drops me and I tumble to the ground. He takes two steps back, his eyes wide with rage and his mouth tight with pain. I spin on my heel, and come crashing into two hard forms. I scream with frustration and kick out, but it's pointless. The tall dark man has my shoulders and, in his grips, I can't move.

Dimitri storms over, taking hold of me and spinning me around. "Will you not learn?" he demands.

He nods to the tall dark man, and in a second I find myself being dragged to the bed. The man drops me onto it, and lifts my arms, raising them above my head and handcuffing me to the headboard.

I lose it.

The feeling of being tied and restrained has everything coming back. It has all those fears I had locked away raising their ugly heads. I scream loudly, and twist my body, trying to avoid his grasps as he takes my ankles.

"Let me go," I screech. "Please don't tie me up. Please, I'm begging you. I'm sorry, please let me go."

Tears tumble down my cheeks, and I close my eyes, shoving back the memories that threaten to rise.

"Stop screaming. If you scream, I'll only make it hurt."

I shake my head from side to side, murmuring words I don't even understand. I tug my wrists—nothing. I tug my ankles—nothing. I screech again, pleading, begging, knowing that I make no sense.

"Silence," Dimitri orders.

"Please," I sob. "Don't tie me up. Please don't tie me up."

He begins to walk toward me, his expression angry, when I growl, "Don't come near me. Please, not while I'm restrained. Don't. Please. *Don't.*"

His eyes flicker with something I don't recognize. It's almost like . . . he understands.

"I told you what would happen if you tried to escape," he hisses, clenching his fists like he's trying to hold back.

"Please, I won't do it again. I beg of you, undo me. Please."

"I can't do that," he says in a hoarse whisper before turning and walking toward the door.

"Please!" I scream so loudly it hurts my own ears. "Don't do this to me. I can't breathe like this. Please . . . don't . . . don't tie me . . . please . . . I'll do anything, just don't tie me."

His body flinches, but he doesn't turn back. He simply orders the two men to watch me, and then he steps out and slams the door.

And I break down.

CHAPTER THREE

Dimitri

I can hear her screaming, and the sound pierces my heart. I want to fuckin' go in there and stuff something in her mouth, but more than that, something inside me is urging me to let her go. The screams, they're not just those of a prisoner. I've had prisoners, and this one is different. She's not afraid; she's been strong, and tough, and mouthy. Then I tied her.

And she broke.

Like me.

Broken.

Was it that bastard Hendrix? Did he hurt her? Rape her? Tie her in a cell? Is that why she's so afraid? Her cries are those of a damaged person. Of a person who has lived through that kind of soul-crushing pain. Her eyes were frantic, darting around, pleading with me to let her go. I wanted to, for a small moment, but then I remembered why I have her, and I knew I had to walk away.

I can't grow soft.

It's not an option.

I close my eyes, lifting my crystal glass to my lips and shooting back the straight whiskey. Fuck her for making me question myself on the first day. That's what she's done. She made me question this entire plan. She's not his lover—that much I have figured out. But she's important to him; I saw it in his eyes. She's not his kid, she's too old. Maybe she's a niece, or a friend. There's a story there, a story that has made a connection.

I will play on that connection.

I turn and storm across the room, walking to the window and opening it. I shove my face out and try to control my breathing the best I can. I push the panic down, the seizing feeling in my chest, the way my head spins, the way my breathing suddenly becomes difficult. *Fuckin' control it, Dimitri. Don't break now. You're better than this, stronger than this. You can't let this shit beat you.*

Goddammit.

I can't let them win.

CHAPTER FOUR

Jess

My wrists are bleeding, I'm exhausted, and there are no tears left; yet I'm still tugging. Still pulling my wrists with a desperation that is consuming me. The more I think about it, the more panicked I become. I tug and I tug, frantic to release myself. I can't stay like this—if I do, I'll go crazy. I can't stand being restrained.

"If you pull those restraints again, I'll flog you so hard you won't walk."

My foster father, Roger, used to make a point of tying me up. At the very thought of him, my body shudders. Nothing in the world could send me over the edge more than the thought of him. His cold hands. His smelly body. The way he used to take what wasn't his. I was helpless, too small to fight. He made sure I couldn't. These binds around my wrists only take me back to that dark place.

I'm glad he's dead.

I hear the door creak, and I snap my head up to see Dimitri standing in the opening, staring at me. He has a crystal glass in his hand, filled with an amber liquid. He narrows his eyes when he sees the blood running down my wrists. With a curse, he puts his glass down and walks in, stopping beside the bed. He peers down at me, and I can see his dark eyes are heavy. He's drunk.

My heart feels like it stops beating.

"Don't look at me like that," he rasps. "I'm not goin' to rape you."

I swallow and close my eyes, turning my head away. I feel him tug on my restraints, and a moment later, my wrists are free. I sob loudly, and as soon as my ankles are free, I roll to my side, tucking my knees to my chest.

"What happened to the girl with the fight?" he says, his voice husky. "What broke you?"

I move my gaze up so I'm looking at him. "I'll never give you the things that break me, jackass."

His eyes flash with anger, and his jaw tightens as he leans down and takes my shoulder, pulling me up. "We're going to clean your wrists and then your nose."

The way he says that tells me it's not an option.

"I'd rather do my own nose. I'm a nurse and I trust myself more than I trust you," I say, my voice determined.

He stares at me but he doesn't argue.

As soon as I'm on my feet he takes me out of the room and down a few long halls until we reach a sitting room. There's a fire going, and a light crackling sound fills the air. I shiver as he leads me over to a maroon settee and shoves me down onto the soft couch. I don't move as I watch him walk over to a cupboard and pull out a small medical kit. He walks back over and sits in front of me, not meeting my gaze.

He reaches down and lifts my wrist, placing it in his big hands. I stare at him, just watching the way his hair drops over his face as he begins to dab the blood off my skin. I notice then the scars on his knuckles—there are a ton of them, all faded. I peer down and squint. He's got light bruising too. Where did he get that? Does he fight a lot? I lift my eyes when I feel him stop cleaning, to see him staring at me. My cheeks heat and I turn away.

"You always stare at people like that?" he asks, beginning cleaning again.

"You always steal people?" I retort.

He snorts. "No, only when I need to."

I shake my head. "You're wasting your time."

"What did I say to you earlier? Ain't your business what I'm doin'."

I fall silent and watch as he continues to clean my wrist. When he turns it over, and finds the deep gash I made, he growls. "What were you thinkin'? You could have killed yourself."

"I don't like being tied," I say in a small voice.

"I can see that," he grumbles. "But pulling and tugging ain't gonna change it."

"Maybe I wanted to make it hurt."

He lifts his eyes, and stares hard at me. "Now why would you want to do that?"

"The pain is better than the memories."

His stare holds mine for the longest moment, then he turns back to what he's doing.

"You're done. I won't tie you again tonight, but if you smart-mouth me any further, I'm not sure I can keep my word on that."

I don't answer him, I just watch as he packs up his kit and stands. I slowly rise, utterly exhausted. I don't have it in me to argue tonight. I just need to rest.

Dimitri finishes up and takes me back to my room. We don't say anything else—what is there to say? I'm nothing more than a pawn in his twisted game and he's nothing more to me than my captor. It's better if we keep everything as a closed book.

The minute we get back to the room, he opens the door, pushes me inside, and closes it without so much as a peep. I sigh and turn.

Not bothering to shower or change, I just flop onto the bed and roll on the soft comforter, pulling it with me until I'm wrapped like a cocoon. Then I close my eyes and everything quickly fades, taking me to a far happier place.

CHAPTER FIVE

Jess

The next morning comes like a bad cold. I open my eyes, remember where I am, and groan. I roll on the bed until I'm propped on my side. The moment I move, I feel my nose throbbing—I know it's not broken, I've seen and felt many during my time as a nurse, but it sure as hell came close. I stare around the slowly brightening room. The sun hasn't been up long, and I can hear birds chirping outside. I stare over at the bathroom door, and my heart pounds. I've been thinking about that spa in there and knowing I'd pretty much kill for an hour in it.

I climb out of the bed and my wrists ache as I move them. I shudder, remembering being restrained last night. It's not something I wish to happen again. One thing I don't like is not having control over my own body. I need to have my own back, and when I'm restrained that is taken away from me, leaving me completely helpless.

I reach the bathroom and shove the door open, staring in. It's a gorgeous room and, by the looks of it, barely touched. I eye the spa bath and I feel myself smile. Don't get me wrong, it's not the most ideal situation, but the fact is that I've spent a long time with a dingy shower and very minimal products. This bathroom is loaded with things I've never even heard of before.

I shove the door closed and step in. I remove my clothes quickly, then lean over and turn the spa on. I go through the range of soaps, and end up settling on a lavender-scented bubble bath. I pour some in, and the bubbles rise up along with the steam. Mmmm. I step over the side and slowly lower into the hot, fresh water.

I'll admit in that moment, I do moan. Loudly.

It's completely called for.

I soak for a solid ten minutes, just enjoying the feeling of the water surrounding me. When I finally sit up, it's because I know I have to attend to my hair. I take a bottle of shampoo and fill my palm. I wash my hair twice, and then put some conditioner in and lean back down to soak. I'm enjoying the water when I rub my foot up my own leg and have a mild heart attack.

Holy freaking hairy legs.

I sit up, glancing around quickly for a razor. God, I've not spent enough time taking care of myself. It's not something I prioritized on Hendrix's ship, being that I was always busy with everyone else. I find a razor and shove the plastic wrapping off it before throwing my leg out of the bath and running it over until it's silky smooth. Then I repeat the process on the next. I attend to my underarms and any other stray hairs that have felt the need to pop up on my body since the last time I eliminated them.

When I'm finished, I climb out and pull on a robe hanging on the door before taking a brush and starting the frustrating process of detangling my hair. I'd been in that stupid cell for a few days, and in that time my hair created its own breeding nest. There are clumps of hair that have stuck together and so many knots my arm hurts after only the first section.

By the time I get through it, it's flowing down around my shoulderblades and, even though it's still wet, it looks good enough. I stare at myself in the mirror. My nose is . . . ugh . . . gross. It's slightly bruised and puffy, and with my puffy red lip beside it,

I really don't look good, but I'm thankful it's not broken. I pinch my cheeks a few times, trying to get some color into my pale skin. I'm blessed with the kind of skin that burns over the mere thought of the sun.

"Out here!"

I hear pounding on the bathroom door and Dimitri's angry voice.

He would scare most people, but it would take a lot more than an angry man on a mission to frighten me. I don't truly believe he will hurt me. I can't explain how I know that, I just . . . do. I swing the door open to see him standing wearing a pair of black jeans and a tight gray tee. He jerks when he takes notice of me, and I'm pretty sure it's because I no longer look like I've been dragged from the streets.

"Fuck," he murmurs.

"Good morning to you too, sunshine." I smile sweetly, walking past him. "You're such a treat to wake up to."

I'm almost sure I hear him mumble something about my hair, but I don't hear enough to know if it's a good comment or a bad comment. It's enough to have me running my hands over it to make sure I haven't missed something. I take a seat on the bed and stare over at him as he picks up a bowl of fruit he's clearly placed down, and hands it to me. I take it, grateful.

"We need to talk," he says.

I raise my brows. "Is that your request or mine?"

He glares at me. "Don't be smart."

I ignore him, lifting a grape and tossing it toward my mouth. It misses completely and lands on the floor behind me. I give Dimitri a coy smile, and lift another one, attempting it again only to have it end the same way, diving to its death on the floor.

"Where is Hendrix docking?" he asks.

I shrug, picking up a piece of pineapple and popping it into my mouth. "I don't know. Where do you think he's docking?"

If you could hear teeth grind, you'd hear Dimitri's. I hide my smile.

"What makes you think you can smart-mouth me, and I won't do something about it?"

I look up at him. "Are you going to do something about it?"

"Don't put it past me."

"Noted."

His face hardens and his body is rigid.

"What kind of technology is on Hendrix's ship?"

I shrug again. "I'm just a whore, remember?"

He slams his hand down on a table beside him. "Just fucking answer my question."

"Say please," I say, throwing a grape into my mouth.

"Fuck," he growls, leaning in closer. "Just. Answer. Me."

I put another grape into my mouth and bite it. To my horror, it explodes sending a squirt of juice right into his eye. He jerks backwards, rubbing at it. I can't help it; I don't want to laugh, but it's one of those moments—there's no stopping it. I press my hand over my mouth and smother my giggle.

"Jesus," he roars. "Are you always so frustrating?"

"I told you that you took the wrong girl," I point out between giggles.

"Answer my questions, or I'll tie you back up. Is that what you fuckin' want?"

"Your threats don't work, you bossy-ass pirate wannabe."

His brows shoot up. "What did you just call me?"

"I didn't stutter," I smirk.

"Firstly, what did I say about you callin' me a pirate?"

I roll my eyes. "Okay, Mr. I Steal Girls, Play On Ships, And Fuck Up Bad Guys But I'm Not A Pirate."

His jaw tics. "Watch it."

I huff. "Or what?"

He ignores that question. "What kind of technology does Hendrix have on his ship?"

"I don't know because I never went into the navigation office."

He sighs angrily.

"What kind of weapons does he have?"

"Well, you know . . . the usual."

He glares at me.

"Guns, what do you think he has?" I snort. "Toy swords? Jesus, ask a real question."

He puts a hand over his face, running it down slowly. I can see he's clearly trying to gather his control.

"Bombs? Knives? Swords? Cannons?"

I raise my brows. "All of the above . . . maybe?"

"What do you mean, maybe?"

"I worked as a nurse, Dimitri. I didn't pay attention to all of that."

"Jesus," he mutters. "Fine, just tell me what you do know."

"He is a pirate."

"For fuck's sake!" he bellows. "Stand up."

I do as he asks, only because his voice is so icy it actually has me reconsidering my sarcasm.

"Now, I'll ask once more. You don't answer me, I'll put you on that bed and shackle you for the entire day. If you piss yourself, it won't be my problem."

"You're a piece of work!"

He shrugs. "I'll do what I have to do. Now, I'll ask one more time. Tell me what you know about Hendrix."

I take a deep breath and know I have to word this just right. I don't want to give too much away.

"Hendrix is a pirate." He opens his mouth to argue, but I continue. "He's the best there is. He knows that ship like the back of his hand and, better yet, he knows the ocean equally well. He's got the best tracking systems there are and he's got a good supply of weapons. He knows all the islands back to front and he's got great contacts at all the docks. That's all you'll get from me."

Dimitri nods stiffly and turns, walking toward the door.

"No 'thank you'? Really?"

He makes a grumbling sound and steps out, slamming the door behind him.

Damn, he's a hard one to break.

CHAPTER SIX

Jess

Two days I've been at Dimitri's house, and in that two days I've spent most of my time in the room. I'm not complaining, it's been nice to be able to catch up on some much needed rest— though, while resting, I think a lot about Hendrix and how I can make sure he doesn't get hurt. It's hard when we're on land. If we were on the ocean, I would be able to plan; here, I've got nothing.

Dimitri has taken me into the library once, where he let me read while he worked. This surprised me, but I didn't argue. I love to read and it gave me a chance to watch him. He's a solid worker, his voice stays one tone when he's working, and he doesn't stray, not even when his pretty maid comes in and offers him beverages. Not only does she offer him beverages, she also adds cleavage to the deal.

I'm sitting by the window today, just staring out at the beautiful gardens. I've read almost all of the readable books in the house, which is a whole of about two, so now I'm spending my time wandering around completely restless. The more I sit, the more I think. I don't like thinking, it only upsets me. I can't let my shell crack, because if it does, Dimitri will see what really lies beneath the surface.

"Mary is gettin' you some new clothes, I need your size."

I hear Dimitri's voice and turn to see him standing at the door.

"Maybe I'd prefer not to wear clothes."

His face doesn't even flinch.

"Really? Not a smile? Nothing? No twitch down below?"

His brows raise.

"Jeez Louise, someone needs to loosen up. I'm a size four."

His eyes travel down my body, before lifting back to my face. "Figured."

"Are you saying you've thought about my size?"

He sighs and shakes his head. "I know women."

"Obviously not well enough, because you had to ask me."

There go those grinding teeth.

"We're done here. I'll have some clothes brought for you."

"Why?" I ask as he's turning.

He doesn't look back at me, but he does say, "Because you're likely to be with me a while. It's not going to be easy getting Hendrix where I want him. It gets cold. You can't live in only what you're wearing."

Then he steps out and leaves me with a slightly hanging mouth.

He's looking after me. He might not admit it, but he is.

I can't help but smile.

~

"Get up."

I hear a voice, but my mind is refusing to come around so quickly. It must be midnight, it has to be—I went to bed around ten and I know I haven't been sleeping long. I groan and I shift my stiff, overly warm body. I'm still wrapped in my cocoon and there is some serious heat trapped inside it.

"Move it, we have to go."

I blink my eyes open, only to see it's definitely still dark. I shove the blankets off and reach up, rubbing my eyes. Why am I being woken in the middle of the night? At least, I think it's the middle of the night. For all I know, I might have only been asleep for an hour or thirty minutes.

"Go?" I croak.

A hand curls around my upper arm and pulls me up.

"Everything I do, you'll do with me. I don't trust anyone as much as I trust myself. Something has come up, and I have to attend. You need to come with me."

"What time is it?" I groan, rubbing my head as Dimitri pulls me from the bed.

"It's three a.m."

I sigh. Well, at least I slept for longer than I thought.

"What could be so important at three a.m.?" I ask groggily as he leads me down the hall.

"None of your business."

"Of course it isn't," I mutter.

Dimitri leads me quickly through the house, taking hold of a coat just before we exit the front door. He tosses it at me, and I wrap it around myself. There's a cool breeze out tonight, and it causes a shiver to rush through my body. I hurry quickly to Dimitri's SUV and there I see the two guards are waiting.

Don't they ever sleep?

The dark-skinned one opens the door for Dimitri. "Are you ready?"

"Ready. Let's go," Dimitri says sternly, before slipping into the driver's seat.

I am shoved into the back and my body protests angrily. I'm tired, my knees are wobbly, and my eyes are drooping. I rest my cheek on the glass window, and my eyes drop closed as the car jerks to life. I very vaguely hear the discussion going on between the men, but I don't care to figure out what it is they're talking about.

I'm exhausted.

It's not okay to be dragged out of bed this early.

We drive for about an hour before coming to a stop at an old warehouse. This particular warehouse is at the end of an alley and is crawling with people. Who in their right mind is awake at this time willingly? Dimitri stops the car and leaps out, bouncing side to side like he's hyped up full of energy. I stare at him with a look of confusion.

"You stay by my side," the guard says. "If you try to run, it won't end well."

"So I hear," I mumble, following him as he moves inside behind Dimitri.

Dimitri is let inside as though he's a VIP. I stare around the massive warehouse as we jostle our way through the people, and I'm quite surprised. It's in good condition. There are lights on the ceiling that are so bright I have to squint. The smell of sweat, alcohol, and something quite pungent fills the air. People are yelling, throwing cash around, and bellowing names toward something I can't see.

Dimitri shoves through the crowd until we reach a rear door. He pushes it open and we step inside. I glance around, taking in the small room. It's got a row of long benches and lockers. It seems darker in here after standing in the intense lights outside. Dimitri turns and uses his fist to hit one of the lockers. It pops open and he rifles through it, pulling out a couple of bandages.

"What is this place?" I ask, still quite fascinated.

"It's a fight club," Dimitri answers, unraveling the bandage and then proceeding to wind it back up over his knuckles.

"A fight club?" I dare to say, not really wanting to know the answer.

"People come, they pay, they watch a fight."

"And you're here because . . ."

He turns to me, his eyes deadly. "Because I'm going to fight."

"What?" I gasp, feeling my eyes widen. "Why?"

"I need information. I'm an exceptional fighter. It works."

"How does fighting get you information?"

He grins, but it's not pleasant. "I don't take the money; instead I use the resources of the clubs. The money they gain from me winning my fights is enough for them to tell me what I need to know. It's a win–win."

I stare at him, completely shocked. "You fight for information?"

He shrugs. "Basically."

"Why? It clearly hasn't worked for you or you would have found Hendrix sooner."

His eyes harden. "I never said all the information I get is reliable."

"And you've been doing this for how long?"

He shrugs. "Five years."

I shake my head. "How does one get into a fight club?"

"I was angry, I liked to take it out on things that were getting me into trouble. A friend told me about these fight clubs. I came to one, loved it, got out my frustrations, and decided to keep coming back. I had a talent for it. Then I gained contacts and found out that I could not only relieve my anger, but also get any information I needed. It became my way of tracking down Hendrix."

I frown. "Why?"

He grunts. "Sit down, stop asking questions, and behave while I do this."

Behave?

Seriously?

"What do you think I'll do," I mutter. "Fight my way out?"

He ignores me as he reaches down, lifting his shirt and removing it in one swift movement. My mouth drops open. It takes me a solid three seconds to convince my brain to close it again. Dimitri's body is huge. No, wait, that just doesn't seem like the right way to describe it. It's . . . *epic*. He's a mass of muscle and bronze skin. His shoulders are wide, narrowing down to a set of well-defined and sculpted hips and a killer ass. I bite my lip and look away.

Someone got the good genes.

"Why are you fighting tonight?" I dare to ask.

He turns, tightening the bandages on his hands. His abs flex as he breathes, and I have to force my eyes to stay on his face. I glimpse a tattoo on his chest, right over his heart. It's a pair of bound hands and they almost look 3D. It's quite . . . disturbing. Especially considering that what those hands are bound with is barbed wire.

"There's someone here who knows information about Hendrix. For a good price—say, my winnings—he'll give me that information. These clubs, they all deal with illegal shit. It's not legal what they're doing here, and a lot of the people here have serious links into the . . . shall we say . . . darker side of the world?"

God.

"I don't know what you think you'll find out about Hendrix. He's a smart man, and he's careful," I growl softly.

He narrows his eyes and I can see his jaw flexing with anger. "There is a lot I will find out about him. I can find where he docks, what islands are his, where he spends his time, where he gets his ship stock and his weapons, and, best of all, I can find out his locations."

Now my jaw tightens. "I won't let you hurt him."

"He deserves everything he gets," he spits.

"Why? Because he left you?"

His entire body jerks. "If it was that simple, do you really think I'd go to so much effort?"

"Why don't you blame your mother?" I snap. "She's the one who put you in this position."

He steps forward and his hands are in tight fists by his sides. "Don't you ever fucking talk about my mother again."

"You don't know half of what you think you do. You still think I'm important to him, but I'm not. You still think you can outsmart him—you can't."

He straightens up and spins on his heel, storming toward the door. Running away—*typical*.

Maybe he's more like Hendrix than he knows.

~

The fighting ring is large, square, and fills one full corner of the warehouse. There are hundreds of people hanging around the railings, shoving their bodies through, screaming profanities at the fighters who are waiting to beat each other half to death just for a reward. I guess sometimes desperation is stronger than common sense.

I turn my gaze to Dimitri. He's doing that bouncing side-to-side thing again, and his jaw is tight. His eyes are on the floor, and he seems to be prepping himself up. How bad will this fight be? Will he get hurt? Or worse? I turn to see the guards standing behind me, their faces empty. They show so little emotion. Do they care about him at all? Is there any concern for his well-being?

"Ladies and gentlemen," a voice suddenly comes across a microphone. "Tonight we have two impressive competitors. First, to my left, we have Panther. He's tall, strong, but most of all, ladies and gents, he's angry."

The crowd screams and claps, chanting his name over and over.

My stomach twists.

Panther is fucking scary.

"And we have an old favorite. We have all put our money into this man before and won, so put your hands together for Dimitri."

The crowd screams louder, and I feel bile rise up in my throat. The other man, Panther, is huge. He's twice the size of Dimitri, and Dimitri is a massive man. I rub my belly, desperately just wanting to get out of here. I can smell sweat and, scarily, blood. I don't move my eyes off Dimitri as he steps up into the ring, bumping his fists together.

"You all know the rules," the microphone man roars. "Whoever goes down for ten seconds is the loser. You may use any means necessary to bring your opponent down. Weapons are not permitted. Take your places."

Any means necessary? I rub my stomach harder. The vile smell of sweat and blood burns my nose, and I try to close my eyes and inhale to calm myself, but it seems as though it's really pointless. Nothing is making me feel better right now. I need fresh air, I need to get outside. I lift my hand and rub my forehead, feeling a fine layer of sweat there. It's a mix of the fighting thing and the mass crowds. I'm not used to crowds.

"'Scuse me, young lady," an old, husky voice says just as a hand lands on my hip. I flinch. "You're in my way. Perhaps you'd like to go on my shoulders?"

I turn and see a vile, old, disgusting man with a row of rotting teeth. My stomach threatens to erupt. His hand on my hip tightens and I try to tug away, but there's no room to move now that people are closing in around me.

"Hands off," a dark voice booms, and I am thankful to hear Dimitri's guard.

"Just havin' some fun," the old man almost whines.

"Take it elsewhere."

I'm exceptionally grateful in that moment for the big, overly bulky guys behind me. I take a small step back into them, needing to know they're a little closer. I turn my eyes back to Dimitri and see his gaze is on me. His expression is stern and intense. He looks up at his guards, nods, and then he turns his attention back to the fight.

"Are you ready?" the man yells.

The crowd screams and roars, waving money around and chanting both men's names.

"Are you set?"

The screaming gets louder. I press my hands over my ears.

"It's time to fight!"

The crowd starts stomping their feet yelling, "Fight, fight, fight, fight!"

I watch as Panther leaps toward Dimitri the moment they're given the go-ahead, catching him off guard. His fist raises and comes crashing down over Dimitri's jaw. I watch as his head swings to the side and blood splatters out. I press my hand over my mouth, making a strangled sound even though no one can hear it through the deafening noise. God, they're brutal.

Dimitri pulls himself together, and manages to duck the next swing by Panther. He lunges forward, driving his shoulder into Panther's pelvis, sending him hurling backwards. Panther stumbles on his feet for a second, but is soon launching back toward Dimitri, who has blood pouring down his chin.

Watching Dimitri like this, I can see a certain level of wild unleashed in his depths. He's wound up, but more than that, he's angry. His jaw is tight, he's panting, and, if looks could kill, the entire room would be dead. He clenches his fists, and when Panther lunges at him again, he drives his fist upwards, smashing it into Panther's nose so hard his skin splits.

I turn my head away. I've seen plenty of blood, but I don't like it.

I hear screaming, I hear booing, and I hear people suddenly chant, "Dimitri, Dimitri." I dare to turn my head again to see Dimitri lift his foot and kick Panther so hard in the side of the face, the man does a full 360 before landing on the ground with a thump. Dimitri reminds me of an uncaged animal; he throws his body onto Panther and he presses his forearm to his throat.

"One!" the crowd bellows.

My mouth drops open as Dimitri grins down at the man struggling for air on the ground.

"Two!"

God, he's like a crazed beast.

"Three!"

I can't look.

"Four."

I have to look.

"Five."

Panther is going slightly blue.

"Six."

He's gasping for air, and Dimitri isn't budging. He's not even bothered that a man is basically dying under his hands.

"Seven."

God, he's going to kill him. I'm sure of it. I rub my stomach furiously again.

"Eight."

Panther is kicking like a sprayed cockroach. His body is flailing around under Dimitri's, but even his big form isn't enough to shove Dimitri off. He's too clever. He's picked the perfect way to hold him down, using his arm to lock him into place and cut his air supply off enough that his struggles are pointless.

"Nine!"

I press my hands to my face, peeking through my fingers.

"Ten!"

Dimitri lets go and stands, throwing his arms into the air and bellowing loudly.

Holy shit.

He's a machine.

My mouth is hanging open and I'm still staring through my fingers when his eyes turn to me.

And he smiles.

Shit.

I shake my head, sure I didn't just see what I did. Dimitri smiled at me. He doesn't smile. He's darkness. He's Mr. Black. He *doesn't* smile. Which tells me only one thing—fighting is his escape. It gives him a sense of freedom, a sense of control. It likely takes away his pain for a second, and when you're in that kind of pain, you do whatever you can to make it go away.

"Time to go," the guard behind me grunts, shoving me through the crowd.

I lose my footing twice, falling into sweaty, dirty men. It takes us a solid twenty minutes to get to the back room. When we do, Dimitri is already there, pressing a wet cloth against his split and extremely bloody lip. His jaw is bruising. He looks like he's high on life, though. He's bouncing still, from side to side. His eyes are bright and his chest is rising and falling heavily.

"Get your info, boss?" the guard asks.

"Got it, Luke."

Luke, that's what the darker-skinned guard's name is.

"When do we go out?"

"Tomorrow morning. Get the ship ready."

My heart hammers and I turn to Dimitri. "What?" I gasp.

He smirks at me. "It's time we taunt your pirate just a little."

My jaw tightens. "You won't find him."

"I've got leverage," he grins, removing the cloth that's now covered in red. "Of course I'll find him."

"He doesn't deserve this," I snap, sitting on an old, metal bench running along the wall.

Dimitri drops the cloth and comes walking over until he stops in front of me, then he kneels until we're eye to eye. I lose my breath.

"Did I deserve to have my mother taken from me? Did I deserve to be beaten and left alone with nothing?"

I open my mouth, but he cuts me off.

"He was all I had. I believed in that fucker and he left me alone. He just ran away and left me without one person to depend on. He deserves every motherfuckin' thing he gets."

My jaw flexes and I bite the insides of my cheeks to stop myself from saying something I shouldn't.

He narrows his eyes and his fists clench. "Your silence tells me you know I'm right."

"You're not right," I spit, crossing my arms. "Do you think you're the only person in the world who has been let down by someone? Shit, Dimitri, you're not. Pull your head out of your ass and change your life, instead of chasing a sick dream of revenge that will only get you killed."

I shove hard in his chest, sending him stumbling backwards. He lands with a thump on his ass. I get to my feet and shoot him a glare before turning to Luke. "I'm sure we can wait in the car."

He looks at Dimitri, who nods briskly. He's angry, I can tell by the way his jaw is flexing and his chest is rising and falling heavily with every breath he takes.

Luke takes my arm before he has a chance to say anything, and leads me out.

This argument will never have a winner.

CHAPTER SEVEN

Dimitri

I clench and unclench my fists. The urge to drive them into the lockers beside me is so huge I have to breathe myself through it.

That girl is driving me crazy.

She thinks she's got an answer for everything. Shit, she probably grew up with a silver spoon hanging out of those pretty fucking lips. She wouldn't understand what it's like to have your innocence stripped from you.

She has no right to judge me.

Or defend that piece of shit.

∽

Jess

I stand in the cool breeze, shifting from one foot to the other as I wait for Luke to open the SUV so we can get in. He's staring at our surroundings, as if checking to make sure no one is watching. Then, right in front of my eyes, he lets me go and walks around to unlock the front door.

He. Just. Let. Me. Go.

It takes my mind a split second to figure out what I need to do. He's going to come back around in less than a minute. This might be my only chance to run. It's not logical, running into a street and letting myself be seen, but it's better than heeding to what Dimitri wants. I spin on my heel and I run.

Fast.

I hear Luke yell, but I put my head down and I charge toward the road. I don't stop when I reach it; I leap out and cross it, causing cars to skid and screech to stops. Drivers hurl abuse at me, some of them yelling out asking me if I need help. I figure that must be because Luke is chasing me. Most people wouldn't just throw themselves into the middle of a busy street.

I hear Luke bark out a curse, but I don't dare stop and see how close he is. Running quickly warms my cold body, and I pick up speed. I thank God in this moment that I've lived on a pirate ship for years and because of that and the limited amount of choices, I've lived a healthy lifestyle. I'm fit. I run down a footpath heading to a beach. A beach is good because they're almost always dark and I can hide easily. I can feel my heart pounding so hard it's making me feel a little ill inside.

I'm frightened.

If I don't pull this off and Dimitri gets me, I'll pay for it.

I'm just about to cross another road to the easiest beach entrance when Dimitri appears in front of me, quick as lightning. I don't even know where he came from, or how he got to me so quickly. I yelp and skid to the left, hurling myself over a railing that apparently stops people from falling down the long hill to the beach.

I tumble over it, and I hit the ground hard. But I've landed with too much force.

So I roll.

I can feel twigs and sticks scratching into my skin as I tumble down the extremely steep hill. By the time I hit the sand below, my mouth is bleeding and my head is aching. I flip myself over and get to my knees, shoving myself forward and crawling until I'm farther out. My wrists ache, and I worry I've hurt one of them. I push to my feet, only to be slammed back down again by a hard, sweaty, half-naked body.

I land back in the sand with a thump, and a loud "*Oomph*" leaves my throat. Dimitri rolls me, flipping me effortlessly onto my back. His big body covers mine, and even though I can't see him, I know his face is close. I can feel hot puffs of breath tickling my cheeks. I don't enjoy that for long, though. I bring my knee up, and I hit him right in the groin.

He roars and tumbles off me. I don't wait. I lunge forward and scurry as far away from him as I can get. Despite his no doubt aching balls, he is back on top of me in a matter of seconds, shoving my face down into the sand. I choke and splutter as clumps of it manage to find their way into my mouth. God, sand is awful when it's all up in your mouth space.

"Get off me," I scream, then choke. "You son of a bitch."

He grumbles and keeps his hands and body pressed into mine. "That was a stupid thing to do."

"On whose behalf?" I bellow. "Mine or your idiotic guards?"

His body stiffens. I spit profusely on the sand—trying to rid sand, go figure.

"Did you really think I wouldn't take a chance to run if I got it?" I manage.

"Get up."

"I can't, you're on top of me," I point out, sarcastically.

He's off me in a second, but his hand clasps firmly around my wrist. He hauls me up and wraps an arm around my waist, pinning me to his side. Then he shoves us toward the stairs. Those would have been nicer to come down on. I struggle and squirm as we walk, and the moment we get back into the streetlights, I start to scream.

"Help, he's kidnapping me! Help!"

He spins me around quickly with a feral growl, and shoves my head into his bare chest. My mouth crashes against his skin. I can taste his sweat and up this close, his smell is intoxicating. I take the opportunity to let him know what I think of him. I bite him, and I make it a good one. He grunts and jerks my head back by gripping a thick lock of hair. He glares down at me.

"Do that again," he warns, "and I'll return the favor."

He shoves me into the SUV that I only just realized is parked right near us. He doesn't let me go as he slides me into the back seat, jumping in behind me. I glance at Luke who is in the front seat, staring out of the window, his jaw tight.

"Good job, Luke," I say. "I bet Dimitri is so happy he's got you watching his back."

"Shut up," Dimitri barks.

Luke glares at me, but quickly starts the SUV and pulls out. I try to pull myself from Dimitri's grip, but he refuses to let me go. Instead, he reaches over and lifts me with little exertion, pulling me onto his lap. His arm goes around my waist, pinning me there. The other arm goes across my shoulders to stop me being able to struggle. My cheek is pressed to his chest, not my mouth. Smart man.

"Let me go," I mutter, trying to squirm. But Christ, he's strong.

"My guard might have had a careless moment," he murmurs. "I will not."

"I'm not going to jump from a moving vehicle!" I cry through gritted teeth.

It's not a bad idea actually.

He doesn't answer, he just leans back in the seat. If I didn't know better, I'd say that this is a position lovers would sit in after making love. I jerk my body a few more times in a futile attempt at getting out of the wall of muscle surrounding me, but there's no point. He's too strong, too determined, and I'm too exhausted.

I slump, feeling my body go limp. I take a small moment to breathe him in. A man such as Dimitri, no matter how evil, is hard not to admire. He's pure beauty. His sculpted body, his defined face, that thick, luscious hair. It's like he was molded to be put on display, so the entire female race could just admire him. Maybe even get a completely implausible idea of what the male race should look like.

No one is ever that perfect.

Except maybe Hendrix; he's about that perfect. It's probably why Dimitri hates him.

I feel my eyelids going droopy, but I don't want to succumb to my exhaustion. If I do, then I'm basically lying here letting Dimitri hold me while I sleep. That's not my idea of strength. I try to take deep breaths to keep my body full of oxygen, but this doesn't wake it up. I squirm again, at which Dimitri tightens his hold. Dammit. I raise my head, and look up at him. He glances down at me, his blue eyes really, really making my heart do strange things. They are such a light blue, just like the sky.

"Your mouth is bleeding," he says simply. Matter-of-factly.

"So is yours. I guess we've both had a good night."

His mouth tics, and for a second, I'm shocked. Was Dimitri about to smile? His face quickly turns back to stone, and he turns his head away, staring out the window. I lower my face again, and I can feel his heart beating against my cheek. I tilt my head, so my ear is pressed right over it. Boom, boom, boom.

I close my eyes, unable to fight it any longer. I feel my body relaxing, and before I can protest any further about my location, I'm asleep.

In his arms.

This is not going well.

CHAPTER EIGHT

Jess

He lets me sleep until the next afternoon, and I'm completely grateful for that. Well, I am until I wake and the moment I'm fed—just some fruit and yogurt—he's got me up and is ordering me to get dressed. We're going back on the ship.

My heart sinks.

Going back on the ship, for some reason, has me feeling slightly depressed. I don't want to go on the ship, I don't want to go on the water. I want to stay on land and I want to stay here for a good long time. I truly don't understand why I feel like this. Perhaps it's because I've been a prisoner for so long. Not in the literal sense, but in the sense that I've never had the chance to be free and just . . . live. Logic, however, tells me that at least being on the ship, Hendrix has a better chance of finding me.

And for that reason, I don't argue.

In fact, I don't say anything as we move about, eating and dressing. Dimitri is barking orders at Luke and the other guard, and they're obediently doing as he asks. He must pay them a lot of money. By the time the sun is setting on the second day, we're in the SUV heading back to the wharf. As we draw closer, I become noticeably agitated. I don't want to go back on that ship.

"Quit squirming," Dimitri says.

He's sitting beside me, holding my one cuffed hand so I can't jump out. I don't look at him, I just stare out the window. He wouldn't understand. He hasn't been desperately living on a ship for two years, doing everything he can to hide from a life that's less than desirable.

"I thought you liked ships?"

Asshole.

I don't answer him again.

When we arrive, and I see his ship, I gasp. Holy shit. I didn't realize how huge it was. It's a gorgeous ship—large and a dark pine in color. There are rows and rows of windows in the hull, leading up to a glorious deck, with big white flags and some seriously talented craftsmanship. He must have paid a lot of money to get something the size of this. He tugs me out of the car and I see another four cars come to a stop. And slowly, they all pile out. There's a good range of men and women. I'm grateful for the women. Well, that is if they're coming on the ship.

God, I hope they are.

I stare as they begin pulling loads and loads of crates and boxes out of the trailers attached to the vehicles. I gape as I get a glimpse of weapons. Those aren't just any old weapons, they're serious destruction tools. My heart begins to pound for Hendrix and Indi. What if Dimitri carries this plan out? What if he actually kills Hendrix?

I feel sick.

I've never stopped and thought that he might be smart enough and resourceful enough to take Hendrix down. In his world, Hendrix is the best. He's deadly, he's determined, and he's powerful. In Dimitri's world, *he's* the best. If those worlds collide, who will come out on top? What would happen to Indi if something happened to Hendrix?

I tremble as Dimitri pulls me toward the massive ship. I try to focus on it, or anything for that matter. I don't want to think about the position I'm left in. I can't. Because if I think about it, I know I'll be left with only one awful choice. And the sad thing is, for me, it is an awful choice because I don't feel like he deserves it. But if it comes down to it, then I'll do what I have to do.

I'll kill Dimitri myself.

∾

"Dimi," a blond girl smiles, sauntering over to us the moment we get on deck.

I stare at her and I'm envious. She's got this amazing body, like a model. Big breasts, tiny waist, and a perfectly tiny, but curved ass. Her hair is long, thick, and tack straight and her eyes are a deep, devastating brown. And, if that's not enough, she's wearing a shirt that is shoving her breasts out of the top, and a skirt that's so tight and short, I'm a hundred-percent sure she's not wearing panties.

I suddenly feel very average. I mean, when is a red-headed girl ever pretty compared to a busty blonde? I lift my hand and stroke my fingers over my ratty red hair. It hasn't been brushed for two days, and I'm feeling it. I pout. There's absolutely nothing to me. No boobs, no ass. Granted, I'm not fat, but I'm so ridiculously tiny it's unfair. My eyes are too big, too green, and my skin is too pale.

"Livvie," Dimitri says, letting his eyes slowly travel over her body.

I turn my face away, and instead focus on the very blue water.

"Who's she?" Livvie asks.

"She's my business, not yours."

Livvie eyes me as though I'm no more than a pathetic little girl who doesn't deserve to be attached to the arm of what is clearly her man.

"Didn't anyone tell you staring is rude?" I say, giving her a glare.

She straightens and flicks her blond hair over her shoulder. "There's really nothing interesting to stare at, if you ask me."

"I didn't ask you."

"Enough," Dimitri says, his voice stern.

Livvie turns her eyes back to him and, I shit you not, bats her lashes in his direction. "How long until you're rid of *her*?"

"I won't be rid of her; she's staying with me so I can watch her."

Say what? I spin as far as my cuffs will allow and glare up at him. He stares down at me, and with the sun in his face the way it is now, his eyes look even more . . . translucent. He squints and lifts a hand over his eyes, shielding them, before saying, "Don't bother arguing, you already know it won't get you far."

I feel my jaw tighten, but I don't argue.

"So when can I see you?" Malibu Barbie asks, in a whiny voice.

"Tonight. I'll put Bobby on guard and we can finish what we started last week."

God, gross.

Malibu smiles at him, and actually slides her tongue out and presses the tip of her finger against it.

"Really?" I snort.

She shoots me a glare, and sashays over, taking Dimitri's face and kissing him so deeply I look away with a flush. Holy shit. The way his jaw moves when he kisses . . . unforgettable. Malibu tears her mouth away and gives me a smug grin before turning and sauntering off.

"Well, that was an experience. Next time maybe let me go before you shove your tongue down Malibu's throat."

Dimitri is just tugging me toward the main room, when he stops and turns. He gives me a skeptical look. "Malibu?"

"You know? Malibu Barbie?"

There goes that lip twitch again.

"Well, Barbie or not, she fulfills her purpose here."

"I just bet she does. She's probably very used to being filled."

Dimitri makes a choking kind of sound, but because we're walking, and his back is to me, I can't see if he's smiling or if he's grunting with annoyance.

He leads me down the first set of stairs, and I am vaguely aware of the layout. I don't remember a great deal, but it's familiar enough. He swings the door to what I guess to be his room open, and takes me inside. Wow. It's far bigger than Hendrix's room, like, twice the size. But then, his ship is twice the size. There's a massive king-sized bed in the middle, and every piece of furniture is expensive. Most of it is wooden.

Dimitri walks me over to the bed and pushes me down onto it, before cuffing my wrist to the headboard. I gasp and tug. "You cannot keep me cuffed to a headboard."

"You'll be there while I'm busy, and when I'm not, you'll be let off, but you won't be leaving this room."

"You're a pig."

He raises his brows and then shrugs. "I have things to do, you're just a piece of the plan. I have no purpose to be kind to you."

"Didn't your mother teach you to respect women?"

His eyes instantly harden and he leans down, getting right up in my face. He seems to enjoy doing that.

"You claim to have such decency," I snap. "But you're treating me no better than you were treated. You hate Hendrix so much for leaving you, yet you're no better than him, are you?"

His fists tighten, and his voice comes out gravelly and rough. "You know nothing about my situation."

"I know your entire situation. It's you, Dimitri, who doesn't know about my situation. You're still living in some pathetic fantasy that I'm important enough to make Hendrix do as you want. Maybe you should do your research before taking a person. If you did, you would see my life is the complete opposite to what you think."

He stares at me for a long moment, before lifting his phone from his pocket and punching in a number.

"John, yeah, it's Dimitri. I need information on a girl. I'll pay whatever it takes."

My mouth drops open.

"Yeah, her name is Jessica Lovenox."

"That's not my name," I snap, tugging my wrists.

He turns to me, his eyes narrowing. "What did you say?"

"I said that's not my name!"

"Give me half an hour, John. I'll call you back."

He ends the call and shoves his phone into his pocket, before stepping back in front of me. "What is your name?"

I just stare at him.

"I'll find it out," he threatens.

"Go right ahead, find it out. If you can do that, why are you asking me?"

He growls and turns, storming over to his desk.

"And what makes you think I matter to him?"

"I can read people's eyes, Jessica. He cares about you. I saw it."

I shake my head and sigh. "Not in the way you think."

"Caring is caring, it will push him to do what I need him to."

"You're wrong, he's not going to risk his life, his crew's life or—"

"Or what?" he snaps.

"Or his girl's life."

His eyes widen for a moment with shock, but he quickly covers it. "He cared. That's all I need."

"Would you risk your lover's life for a girl you cared just a little bit about?"

"I care about no one, so yes, I would."

49

I shake my head. "That's exactly what's wrong with your plan, Dimitri. You don't care, so you can't possibly understand it."

"Believe me," he says, turning back to his desk. "He'll come for you, and when he does, I'll be ready."

"You'd take a man away from a woman who has given up her life for him. His lady, she adores him. Does that not bother you at all?"

"I adored my mother, it didn't matter to him when he had her killed."

"Did you ever wonder *why* he had her killed?"

His eyes flare with anger. "Why is of no importance to me—the fact that he did is enough."

I shake my head and turn away.

"There are clothes here for you, I've had some brought in," he begins, just completely passing our conversation off. "You're going to be staying with me. I'm sure you're not stupid enough to jump over the side of a ship, but if you are, then you're signing your own death warrant. Until we're out in the water a good distance, you'll stay cuffed."

I glare at him. "I'm not staying with you."

"You don't get a choice."

I stare over at his bed and then around the room. "Where am I supposed to sleep? Your plan isn't very well thought out. Maybe you should consider reorganizing it before you end up embarrassing yourself," I mock.

He walks over, kneeling on the bed and getting right up in my face. "My plan is without flaw. My bed is big enough for two and I suggest you keep your mouth closed, before I give you a reason to open it."

I gape, my mouth wide open. "I'm not sleeping next to you!"

He looks away, bored. "It's a bed, it's comfortable. Sleep on the floor if you wish."

I tug on my cuffs. They merely rattle, causing the bed to shake just slightly. "Fine by me."

He shakes his head, walking over to his desk. "We'll see how long that lasts."

"What's that supposed to mean?"

He gives me a hard stare. "It means the floor is hard as stone."

I hate being cuffed to his bed, but at least one of my hands is free. I watch as he pulls out his guns and lays them on the desk. Then he throws a phone down and a few pens from his jeans pockets before taking hold of his shirt and lifting it over his head. My eyes widen, and I will myself to look away but I can't. Goddamn that level of perfection. He runs a hand down his abs, then he lifts one up and scruffs his hair before heading to the bathroom.

I just watch.

Shit.

This isn't going to end well.

∼

Dimitri

The hot water runs down over my body.

It's tense, I can feel it in every muscle on every limb. My shoulders are stiff, my head is pounding, and my back aches. I reach around, rubbing my shoulders, trying to ease some of the tension. It's no use. Looks like I'll need to go and find Livvie after all tonight. She has a way of easing my body.

I think about Jess, and my head seems to haze over.

If that's not her name, then what is? If she's not who she says she is, what has she done to feel the need to hide so much of herself?

Curiosity burns, I can't deny it. I've met a lot of women in my time, but never one so determined as she. She's not willing to break, not willing to show a piece of herself that's anything other than hard.

She's just like me, in a sense.

That never makes for a good combination.

CHAPTER NINE

Jess

I stare at his gun. I really want to be able to get to it. Like, I really, really want to. I hate the sick feeling swirling in my belly right now, because it means that I'm actually considering the worst. The worst is killing Dimitri, so that he won't hurt the people I love. I can't let him hurt Indi and Hendrix. Those two have become the only family I know. And I will fight against everything I am to protect that family.

Steam fills the room as Dimitri steps out.

He's got a black towel around his waist. He's got little beads of water trickling down his abs, disappearing into the thin line of dark hair that goes to a place I'm trying very hard not to think about. His hair is still so damp that it's stuck to his forehead and his eyes are almost hazy. He looks relaxed. He's got a bruise forming on his cheek and his lip is a little puffy.

"Why are you staring at me?"

I quickly jerk my gaze up, not looking at him. I know if I do, he'll see the warm flush in my cheeks. I chew on my lower lip and turn my gaze over to him, unable to keep it away. He's watching me, his eyes intense. He looks like a big, brooding piece of man meat that's so damned edible I'm really struggling to remember why I hate him. But I do . . . hate him, that is.

I hate him. I hate him. I hate him. I hate him.

I swallow and turn away, shifting my body so I'm lying down, then I mumble, "Can you please cuff me lower, I don't like having my hands above my head while I sleep."

I hear the floor squeak as he moves, then I feel the heat of his skin as he so openly leans over me, shoving his chest into my face. A drop of water falls and lands on my nose. I really have to hold back the urge to snake my tongue out and lick it off as it rolls down my skin. He uncuffs my arm and moves it down, where he cuffs it again. He seems to linger a moment, before he moves back and straightens.

"Happy, now?"

"Not entirely."

He snorts. "Is there a moment you're not running your mouth off?"

I shrug. "I'm actually usually very quiet, I keep to myself where I can."

He shakes his head. "I doubt that."

I shrug again. "It's true."

"Funny," he mumbles, stepping out of my vision and dropping his towel. I hear it land on the ground. Sit, heart. Sit. "I could have sworn you've not kept to yourself—at all."

"I have no reason to keep to myself. You are trying to take away my family. Even the weakest of us have our time to fight. This is my time."

He doesn't answer me, so I turn my face to see him standing, wearing nothing but a pair of black jeans that he hasn't yet buttoned. His arms are crossed over his chest, and he's got a look on his face that I'm assuming means he's deep in thought. I'm expecting him to argue with me again, but instead he leans down, picking up a shirt from the floor and walking past me.

"Hey!" I yell as he gets to the door. "What if I need to pee?"

He stands a moment, before turning and looking at me with a somewhat amused expression. "Then you yell."

"You can't be serious."

"Deadly," he says, before stepping out of the door.

Great.

Just great.

∼

I hear a giggle, and I lift my head from the hard, lumpy pillow to see Dimitri stumble into the room followed by Livvie. Her top has been popped open and her cleavage is on display for the world to see. And it's a perfect cleavage. Perfect. She throws her head back, causing her luscious locks to tumble down her back as she laughs. Dimitri has his arm around her waist. His shirt, too, is unbuttoned.

The minute the bedroom door closes, I lose my light. I hear them shuffle about, and then I hear the sound of kissing.

Oh no.

No way.

I do the only thing I can think of, in that moment. I yell.

"I need to pee!"

Silence fills the room.

"What is she doing in your room?" Livvie whispers.

"Don't trust her in the cells," Dimitri adds.

"Excuse me," I snap. "Pee . . . you said to yell. I'm yelling. I need to pee."

"Fuck sake," Dimitri growls. "Wait here, Livvie."

"You can't be serious? Let's go to my room. Leave her here."

"I can't leave her here," he whispers angrily. "She'll piss on my bed."

"Jesus," I yell, shaking my head. "I'm not a dog."

"Livvie, wait, I'll be back."

I hear shuffling, and then Dimitri is by my side. He uncuffs me and hauls me up. I land in his arms and I can't stop my hands flying out in front of me automatically. They land flat on his chest, my fingers splayed. He smells like whiskey and what I'm guessing is Livvie. He turns me quickly, and shoves me into the bathroom. When the door is closed, I quickly relieve myself.

I hope to God he's not actually going to stay in the room.

That wouldn't be okay.

By the time I get back out, the lights are on and Livvie is gone. I stare around the room, just to make sure I haven't missed her, but she's definitely not there. Dimitri is on the bed, leaning against it.

"Cheers for that," he grumbles, staring at the ceiling.

"For what?"

"For cock-blocking me."

I snort. "Go to her room, I'm sure you can manage."

He doesn't say anything, he just rolls and stands, walking toward me with a set of cuffs. I put my hands behind my back.

"Why can't I have a decent sleep uncuffed?"

He's already shaking his head, even before I've finished speaking.

"You've run with pirates, which means you know things about the ocean I don't. I don't trust that you wouldn't have a way to escape me."

"My hands hurt," I protest, keeping them behind my back. "Just let me sleep for one night."

He studies me a moment, and then he steps forward. I take a step back. He jingles the cuffs in his hands and then he's lunging for me. His arms wrap around me and my back slams against a nearby wall. I feel his fingers slide down my arms until he takes hold of my wrists. He leans in close, his face inches from mine.

"I'll let you sleep with your hands down."

He spins me around, using my wrists, and he tugs me toward the bed. I'm still catching my breath after his close proximity. He throws me onto the bed and climbs on beside me. He throws the covers back, slides us in and then snaps the cuffs on my wrist. Just as I think he's about to cuff me back to the bed, he reaches his hand over and cuffs the other one on his wrist.

"Seriously?" I gape.

"Your hand isn't above your head, but I'm pleased."

I can feel the heat of his hand against mine and I'm not sure I can make it through an entire night basically holding his hand.

"I said I'd sleep on the floor."

He nods his head toward the ground. "Off you go, then. I won't be uncuffing you, though, so your hand will be in the air. You decide which you want most—a comfy bed or your pride."

The bed is comfortable, but the pillows aren't. If I sleep on the hard floor, with hard pillows, the chances of me sleeping are slim. I grind my jaw and settle in beside him.

"If you touch me, I'll hurt you."

He snorts. "Don't flatter yourself. I have myself a fine woman in the other room."

I feel insignificant now.

"It wouldn't be so bad if you let me brush my hair."

He turns his head and stares at me. "What the fuck are you talking about?"

"I'm not up to standards, because my hair is awful. If I brushed it, I wouldn't look so . . . insignificant."

He narrows his eyes.

"Need more than a brush."

Ouch.

I hate him. Truly.

"You're below the scum of the earth, Dimitri."

"And you're sleeping with me. Those who lie with dogs are sure to get fleas."

"Asshole."

He reaches across and flicks the lights off.

This is going to be a long night.

CHAPTER TEN

Jess

I can feel his hands on my body, the way they slide down. I can't escape him, it doesn't matter what I do. He's always there, always taking away what I don't want to give. I cry out, trying to struggle, trying to just make it stop. His breath is on my cheek, horrible and so dirty. A hand slides up my thigh, dipping under my skirt.

No.

Please, for the love of God no.

I wake up with a scream, my body thrashing from side to side. Big hands are grabbing at me, trying to keep me still. Panic rises and I kick out, wanting to make it hurt. You can't get to me now, Roger. I'm bigger, stronger, better. I'll kill you.

"Jess!"

I shake my head. The voice, husky from sleep, is not Roger's.

"D-Dimitri?" I breathe.

"Shit, are you okay?"

Okay?

I blink a few times, realizing what's happened. My body is drenched with sweat, my hands are shaking, and my emotions are shot. I had a nightmare. It happens a lot. I sit up slowly, realizing my arm is uncuffed. When did that happen? I tremble as I focus on Dimitri, sitting beside me. The light is illuminating his concerned face.

"Shit, you're shaking."

I can't answer, I'm in some sort of shock. He reaches out, putting his hands on my shoulders, causing me to jerk away with a cry.

"Shit, sorry," he says, pulling back.

I blink some more. "I . . . it was just a dream."

"Some fuckin' dream."

I nod, looking away. He gets out of the bed and walks into the bathroom, returning a moment later with a glass and washcloth. He hands the glass to me and I take it gratefully, sipping the cool water inside. He shoves the washcloth in my direction. "You're sweating real bad."

"Oh," I say, taking it. "I'm sorry."

He shakes his head. "Don't be, it ain't your fault you dream."

I wipe my face, closing my eyes as the calming cool fills my body. That's better. So much better.

"I can sleep on the floor, I know it probably bothers you," I say, daring to look up at him.

"We all dream. I know what it's like."

A strong silence falls between us and our eyes remain locked. I turn away quickly, swallowing. "It sucks."

He snorts. "Yeah, it does."

"It'll probably happen again, Dimitri. I dream a lot."

"Join the club," he says, taking the washcloth from my hands. Our fingers graze and I shiver, feeling so vulnerable in this moment.

"Milk," he says, his voice low. "It helps. You want some?"

I nod and he gets out of the bed, disappearing from the room. That was strange. I sit, tucked up in a little ball, until he returns with a mug of milk. He hands it to me, his eyes watching mine as I take it and sip it. The warm milk eases my throat and stops the aching in my body.

"Thanks."

He nods, turning away. "Try and sleep, yeah?"

"Yeah."

I watch him go to his desk, and if I didn't know better, I'd say Dimitri just showed me kindness.

～

An entire week passes, and with each day that goes by, I feel myself slipping. My witty cover-up is becoming weaker and weaker. I'm scared. I can't stop thinking about Hendrix and Indi. If something happens to them, I'll never forgive myself. It's on me to make sure it doesn't, but Dimitri isn't budging. He makes me walk with him all day every day, not uncuffing me except to let me shower and eat. It doesn't matter that we've had small moments between us.

He doesn't trust me.

I get that, but it makes it difficult for me to find a way to end this. Just the thought of that has my stomach coiling. You can't sleep next to someone each night, and begin to feel what they're about, then just kill them with no emotion. Dimitri has pulled an emotion from me, and that emotion is confusing and all consuming. And I have to kill him. I have to. There is no choice. If I don't, I'm risking my family.

I don't know how I'm going to do it, though.

But I have to. Somehow.

"You're going back to the room," Luke says, tugging my arm and bringing me back to right now—I've been living in my own head a lot lately. "I have work to do and babysitting isn't part of my job description."

"I know that," I mutter, as he pulls me along. "You didn't do a very good job last time you were left to babysit me."

He grunts, but continues dragging me to the door. Dimitri left me with Luke after supper tonight, and disappeared with Livvie.

We all know what he's doing with her, and I'm not sure that sits well with me. Worse, I don't even know why it doesn't sit well with me. Luke has been grumbling for the past two hours, and he's finally decided he's sick of looking after me. I don't blame him really, I'm tired of being led around like a damned dog because Dimitri won't let me drop these stupid cuffs.

"He's busy," I point out just as we step below deck. I was enjoying the fresh, salty air.

"Not my problem."

He takes me to Dimitri's door, and the moment we get to it, he grips the door handle and flings it open. No knocking. No letting himself be known. Nope, he just swings that sucker open as though he owns the place. I'm scared to look in, because I know who and what Dimitri has been occupying his time with. I gasp when I finally get the courage to look. I see Dimitri on the bed with Livvie. He hasn't heard the door open, probably because she's moaning so loudly. He's pounding his cock into her deep, her legs are over his shoulders and the look on his face is completely expressionless. I press my free hand to my chest and struggle to breathe.

I can't move, though.

Clearly Luke can't either because he hasn't taken my arm and pulled me away.

We watch as Livvie reaches up, going to rest her hands on Dimitri's chest. He jerks his body, his face scrunching in utter disgust, and then suddenly his hands are curling around hers, shoving them above her head forcefully. "You know the rules—no touching me with your hands. You don't get to feel."

I turn my eyes to Luke, who is smirking. He's finding this . . . funny? He's watching his boss fuck Malibu Barbie and that's somehow amusing? I feel my cheeks burning and my heart pounding as I turn back to Dimitri and Malibu. She's trying to press her lips to his chest now, as if she didn't hear him tell her no. He lets go of one of her hands and grips her jaw so tightly she yelps.

"What. Did. I. Say. About. Touching?" he growls.

"Jesus, Dimi!" she snaps, jerking her face away. "You never let me touch you during sex."

He shoves off her suddenly, sending her body sailing off the bed. I catch a glimpse of his cock and holy shit—holy fucking shit—it's huge. With flaming cheeks, I turn and try to rush off. Only to realize Luke still has my cuffs. I stumble and trip over my own feet, crying out loudly. Luke jerks me back up by my chains and when I look back into the room, Dimitri is staring at us.

"Enjoying the show, Luke?" he grunts, but I can see the anger in his face.

I'm not looking at him, I'm looking anywhere but at him.

Luke snorts and shoves me forward. "Think your girl here was enjoying it more; I could nearly hear her pussy clenching."

"You jerk!" I snarl as he shoves me into the room.

"Take her," he says, his tone bored. "I'm done babysitting. Get Wiley to do it."

Wiley is the other guard-slash-asshole Dimitri has following me around when he doesn't want to. Though Wiley is a little kinder and more talkative than Luke. Without waiting for Dimitri's answer, Luke turns and walks out. I can feel my cheeks flaming. He just left me in a room with a naked couple whose sex was just disrupted. That's not awkward, no, not at all.

"Get out, Livvie," Dimitri orders, his voice still thick.

"Goddammit, you're never going to finish satisfying me. That girl is always around," she grumbles, tugging on her panties as though I'm not standing in the room.

I dare to look at Dimitri, no doubt expecting him to be staring at Malibu's boobs, but he's not—no, he's looking at me. His eyes are trained on my face. Every now and then they slide down to my lips. God, if he keeps looking at me like that, I might offer to take Malibu's place beneath him. I swallow, inwardly cursing, and turn my gaze back to my feet.

I need new sneakers.

Really, really need new sneakers.

"Move it," Dimitri barks.

"I'm moving," Malibu snaps. "Jesus."

She storms past me, half dressed. I don't miss the moment when she rams her shoulder into mine. I grind my jaw and try to hold back the string of curse words I'd like to spit at her. When the door slams, I stare up at Dimitri again. He's still looking at me. Why is he still looking at me? God, have I got something on my face? No, that look isn't one of humor, it's a little bit . . . lusty.

"I, uh, sorry, I, uh, walked in and . . ."

Get it together, Jess.

"I didn't mean to ruin your night."

He's silent for a long moment, so I look at him again. He's still staring. Honestly. Maybe he's having a brain aneurism and I just don't know about it.

"No problem," he says, and damned if his voice isn't thick with need. "She doesn't do as she's told anyway."

I snort. "Well, it's not surprising, since last time I checked she isn't a dog."

His eyes harden and he glares at me. "I have one rule, it's not hard to follow."

I sigh, walking in the room and rattling my cuffs in his face. "I need to shower. Take them off."

"You're not curious about that rule?" he says, digging into his jeans and pulling out a key.

"Not really. Should I be?"

He shrugs and when his hands touch mine, I can't help the shudder that runs through me. He lifts his eyes, even though his hands are still working. They meet mine and I can see full awareness in them. He knows I just shuddered, and worse, he knows why.

"Are you going to fuck me?"

"W-w-w-what?" I gasp, shaking my head quickly.

"It's a simple question."

My mouth drops open. "I'm your captive, I'm sure there's a condition created for the love between a captive and a captor."

He tilts his head to the side, studying me. "Stockholm syndrome, and you don't have it."

"How would you know?" I say, crossing my arms.

He gives me an expressionless, almost bored look. "Your arousal is very real."

I gape, giving him a fully disgusted expression. "What?"

"You heard me—I can almost smell it on you. All it would take for me is one swipe of my tongue through that sweet pussy and you'd be on your knees. Now, answer my question."

I shake my head. "I don't think so, buster. And what makes you think I have a sweet pussy—I could be a man."

He snorts. "You're not."

"I could be," I whisper as he steps closer, getting far too close to my comfort bubble.

"You're not."

"It's a very real possibility."

"Not."

"Okay, so even if I'm not . . ." I begin, struggling for breath as he stares at my lips. "You still don't know I have a sweet pussy."

"You have a sweet pussy."

"You can't possibly know that!"

His mouth jerks up at the corner, and I nearly fall to my knees.

"You. Have. A. Sweet. Pussy."

"You're such an asshole, I hope you're aware of that."

He tilts his head and gazes at my neck like he wants to lunge at it and suck it.

"I'm aware," he murmurs.

"Take a step back," I order, my voice shaky.

"Answer my question."

"W-w-what question?"

He steps forward again, leaning in so close I can actually smell Malibu's perfume on him. Ugh.

"Are. You. Going. To. Fuck. Me?"

"Dream on," I whisper, unable to force my voice to make an appearance.

He smirks. Goddamn him. I've not seen anything but a hard expression on his face, so seeing him smirk is kind of like seeing sunshine. I stare at his lips—oh, they're so full and manly. And when he's smirking, I can see a dimple. Just one, though. Strange man.

"Then my one rule won't matter to you, will it?"

I shift nervously. "I suppose not."

"We'll see."

"Can I shower now?"

He steps back, waving his arm toward the door. "By all means."

I rush off, getting to the door and taking hold of the handle. Just as I reach it, I turn and open my mouth before I think about it.

"Do you have some kind of . . . condition?"

He raises his brows.

"I mean, you're one thing one minute, and another the next. I thought maybe . . ."

"Maybe I just like a challenge."

I study his face. He's serious. He thinks I'm a challenge. A challenge for what? To get into bed? Is he trying to get into my panties because I'm fragile? I turn my expression to stone, and he notices. Boy does he notice. His whole body stiffens and he narrows his eyes.

"Don't bother," I growl. "You'll never have sex with me, I can assure you of that."

"Care to tell me why?"

I look him dead in the eye. "I imagine for the same reason you won't let anyone touch you."

I close the door, but not before I catch his expression.

It's one of complete shock.

Yeah, buddy. I told you I wasn't what you thought.

CHAPTER ELEVEN

Dimitri

The same reason as me.

The same reason *as me.*

No, it's not possible. She's read me all wrong. She would have no idea why I don't like being touched, she's *just assumed.* She couldn't know. Nobody knows. Nobody understands what it's like being me. All that's happened here is that she's attempted to piece together a story as to why I am the way I am.

I'm used to it.

Many people in my life have tried to figure me out. Countless psychologists have spoken to me, trying to get to the roots of who I am. No one ever gets deep enough—I won't allow it. The shell of me is what I am, and that's how I intend it to remain. Some pirate's whore won't allow me to change my mind.

I should have never given her a minute of myself, not a damned minute.

Now she thinks she knows. And now she'll try to play on that. No, that can't happen. I won't let it happen. I've lived too long being the only thing I have. I have women, they respect my boundaries—mostly. I have my men and my missions. There is only one goal in my life, one thing that I keep breathing for—revenge. Nothing will come in the way of that.

And yet it did. For just a second I forgot what it was I wanted so badly.

Never again.

~

Jess

Another week later.

You've got to be kidding me. No way. No freaking way. Why would she choose this exact moment to show up? I mean seriously. I sit on the bed, staring at the door and then back at my hands. I can't tell Dimitri. He doesn't even look at me right now, let alone help me when I need him. Since the night I caught him with Malibu, he's barely acknowledged me.

He even lets me roam the ship now.

My stomach cramps and I bring myself back to now. She's here—Aunt Flo, otherwise known as the Red Sea, Doomsday, the rag, Aunt Cherrie, surfin' the crimson wave, the Red Dragon, Shark Week, or to those of us who are of a more simple mind—period.

Yes, my period is here.

I cup my face in my hands and groan. The two girls that actually came on this ship with us are snotty, rude, and are here for nothing more than to serve Dimitri. They're not going to help me. The best I'd get from them is hurled over the side of the ship to make good of the name "Shark Week." The only chance I have is to go to either Luke or Dimitri. I don't have any kind of protection, being that I was captured and taken against my will. So I have to ask someone.

Luke would laugh at me, he's that kind of evil.

That leaves Dimitri. I don't know any of the other twenty men on this ship, and they've been given strict instructions not to know me. Though one of them gives me a smile that really, really makes me want to go and talk to him. It helps that he's handsome and has the sweetest face I've ever seen.

Back to now, though.

I have to approach Dimitri. Not only that, but I have to ask him for tampons and pads. I groan loudly and rub my cheeks, feeling utterly horrified that my life has resorted to this. Maybe I should throw myself off the ship—it would make for a far more interesting ending than having to ask a man who despises me for womanly protection.

It has to be done, though.

I get to my feet and squirm uncomfortably as my stomach gives me another dull ache. Taking a deep, steadying breath, I walk out of the room and toward the massive dining area. Dimitri spends a lot of his time there, plotting against Hendrix. He's not asked me a lot, which surprises me considering he took me to lure him in. I suppose in the scheme of things, he doesn't need anything from me to do that. Just having me here is enough to get Hendrix out of hiding.

It takes me a solid five minutes to convince myself to enter the dining room. By the time I do, everyone is staring at me. Yes, I'm standing in an open doorway. I look over the men until I see Dimitri, sitting at the end of a long table. He's got Malibu on his lap, and the fact that I can't see his hand and she's making strange faces tells me he's not just talking to her. Great. Just great.

I put my head down and walk over, hating that I am being forced to do this. I clear my throat when I reach him and he slowly raises his eyes until he's staring up at me. "What?" he mutters.

"I . . . I need to speak with you, it's important."

"I'm busy," he says, running his hand up Malibu's thigh.

She's smirking at me, and it's taking all my strength not to let my PMS free and bitchslap her upside the head.

"It's important," I grind out.

"So is what I'm doing right now," he says, bored.

Asshole.

"I don't care what you're doing right now," I snap. "I need to talk to you."

"Later."

"Now would be good."

He stares at me, his expression still bored. "I said . . . later."

"It's important," I force out through gritted teeth.

He leans forward, causing Malibu to squeak. "I said fuckin' later."

I throw my hands on my hips and get up in his face. "What is wrong with you? Did your mother drop you on your head when you were a baby? No, scratch that—she would have had to do it numerous times for it to have created something like you."

I can nearly hear his teeth grinding together.

"You're walking a very fine line."

"What are you going to do?" I scoff. "Sit there in your chair like a tough wiseass? You're pathetic, Dimitri."

"You know nothing about me," he growls, throwing Malibu off his lap and standing.

"I know everything about you. You feel sorry for yourself because of a life you had that was bad. Instead of changing it, you dwell on it until you become *this*." I shove my finger at his chest.

"You know nothing about the man I am, or why I do the things I do. If you want to hate someone for this situation, hate Hendrix."

"Hendrix is three times the man you are!"

I hear a few gasps, and Dimitri lashes out, taking my shoulders and hurling me forward.

"Hendrix is a lowlife scumbag who puts his crew before his family. He will bleed and I will make it slow and painful. If you're lucky, I might let you watch."

"You're a monster. Hendrix won't let you beat him. You want to know why? Because he is a good, strong man who fights for what he believes in."

"Well, he doesn't have very good taste then, does he?"

Ouch.

I shove at his chest so hard he has to take a step back.

"You know what? I hope he makes you pay."

I turn and rush from the room, feeling my hands shaking with rage. Tears finally escape my eyes and tumble down my cheeks. I stumble four times before I reach the stairs to the deck. I rush up them, trembling so hard my teeth are rattling together. I get up on deck, and there's a cool, crisp breeze flowing in. I drop to my knees on the floor, wrapping my arms around myself and gasping for air.

He's a horrible, awful, rotten human being. I don't know why I ever thought he was anything different.

I blink my tears back, trying to clear my vision. They burn their way out before drying on my cheeks. I glance quickly around the deck, making sure I'm not with company up here, but I see it's quiet. The ship rocks from side to side. Usually this wouldn't bother me but my stomach is coiling so tightly it suddenly makes me feel ill. I drop my eyes to the floor and realize I'm actually leaning against a box. It's like a crate. I'm about to look away when I see that there are weapons in that crate. Quickly, without thinking, I lift the lid.

Guns. A shitload of them.

My heart pounds as I reach in and take a .22 out of the box with trembling hands. I run my thumb over the shiny, hard metal and swallow. I stare down at the rest of the guns—there are at least twenty. Someone left this here—this is an accident without a doubt. A man like Dimitri wouldn't leave something like this out for someone like me to find. Someone made a mistake, a mistake that may just save my life.

"Who the fuck do you think you are?"

I hear Dimitri's voice, and I stand quickly, spinning around with the gun raised. It's not exactly what I planned on doing, but now that it's in the air and his eyes are wide, I realize it may have just been the right choice. My hands tremble, not because I can't shoot this gun, but because I know what I have to shoot at.

"You're going to shoot me?" Dimitri says, his voice solid. "Why? Because you can't handle the truth?"

"You," I snarl, "are the one who can't handle the truth."

"Your truths mean nothing to me," he barks.

"Because you know they're right, perhaps?" I whisper.

"If you want to shoot me, Jessica, then shoot me—but before you do, know this: I am doing what I have to do to get my dignity back. It was stripped a long time ago. I don't expect you to understand—how could you? You've never been the child nobody wants. You've never had to fight for your life. You've never lived through what I've lived through. I lived through it because of him. Your words will never change that, and in your mind, you know that."

My hand is shaking now, and my lips are quivering.

"So if you're going to shoot me then do it and hurry it up. I don't have time to waste with pathetic little girls pretending they know how to shoot guns, who don't have the slightest clue what it's like to live in the hard world."

I open my mouth and my words are flowing out before I get the chance to stop them. "I do know what it's like to be the child nobody wants. I know because my parents died when I was just four years old. They left me alone and orphaned. I was shoved through the foster system until one day I was set with a permanent family.

My foster father started raping me when I was twelve years old. I wasn't even old enough for my first fucking period—which, by the way, is all I wanted you for. I have my period and I needed help." I shake my head, stopping the tears, refusing to look at him. "By the time I was sixteen, I'd had enough. I hid a knife under my pillow. When he came in, and he was inside me, pounding my innocence out, I lifted my knife and I stabbed him so many times his face was unrecognizable. I killed him. I ran and somehow ended up on the wharf. Hendrix was there. He saved me from a life of jail and abuse. So, the man you know and the man I know are two very different people."

He's staring at me and, oh God, his expression.

I aim the gun and shoot it just close enough that it grazes past his head. He flinches, but his eyes don't move from mine.

"And if I wanted to shoot you, Dimitri, I could. Easily. That's what pathetic girls with no idea do when they're stuck on a pirate ship because their life and freedom have been snatched from them." I throw the gun on the floor and I turn, walking off. When I reach the door, I twist back and mutter, "Oh, and by the way, my birth name is Blair. Just Blair. It's not overly beautiful or special but it's the only thing left in my life that I can call mine."

My entire body is numb.

So is my heart.

CHAPTER TWELVE

Jess

I hate crying, it makes me feel weak. I gave up any weakness I had in my life a long time ago. I don't have time for weak, I only have time for here and now. I'm trying to remind myself that I am better than this, braver even. It's not working. My hands are trembling, my lip is quivering, and I've got my period, which, mind you, is just putting icing on the cake.

I hear the door squeak open. I don't look up.

Why bother?

I hear shuffling and I feel a presence in front of me. I slowly lift my tear-filled gaze and see Dimitri standing in front of me. He's got a handful of . . . is that tampons? If I weren't so broken, I'd probably laugh at the image of this big, beautiful man with a handful of pink floral tampons. He stretches his hand out, pushing them toward me. I reach up, my fingers still trembling. I take them from him, grateful.

"Th-th-th-thank you."

His eyes are empty; he looks so . . . sad.

He nods and turns, walking back to the door. When he reaches it, he stares over his shoulder at me. He hesitates for a moment, his face tight with emotion. He wants to say something, but he's clearly debating whether it's worth it. With a deep, defeated sigh he finally speaks.

"I had . . . I had no idea that you had such a hard life," he murmurs. "It's hard to tell when you're so put together, so brave. I envy your strength. It's something I lack."

My eyes fill with tears and for a while he stares at them. Then, without any words, he turns and walks out.

Breaking my heart all over again.

CHAPTER THIRTEEN

Dimitri

My chest hurts.

It fucking hurts.

It feels like someone has reached in and torn my heart into a thousand tiny pieces. Everything up until this exact moment in my life is now a blurred mess. I thought I was the way I am because of the incidents that happened in my life. Then I found out about her. She's had an equally hard life, yet she's so focused on fixing things, so focused on making herself a good person.

Where did I lose that?

Revenge is all I've breathed for the past ten years. Now she's making me question my sanity. She's making me question everything I am. I've never, not for one second, questioned if I was doing the right thing. In my mind, it was and is the right thing. People who cause other people pain and suffering should have the same in return.

I grip the side of the ship, panting. Is it weakness? Is that why I've not turned out the way she did? Am I too consumed with myself to see beyond that? I envy her; my entire body aches with it. She's managed to pull herself out of a situation and create inner peace for herself. She's given herself the one thing I've been searching for, for as long as I've breathed.

Peace.

Never, in my wildest dreams, did I ever think one woman would change everything I've worked so hard for within the space of ten minutes.

Where the fuck do I go from here?

~

Jess

I step up onto the deck and I see him, standing in the corner, gripping the railings so hard his fingers look like they're straining. I take a step toward him, not fully understanding why I'm even here. He's cruel, and awful, and . . . shit . . . he's broken. If anyone understands broken, it's me. I walk over quietly. He's hanging his head, his long, thick hair falling over his face.

My heart breaks a little more for him.

I reach out when I get to him, and with trembling fingers I put my hand on his shoulder. Everything moves quickly after that. He spins around so fast I'm sent stumbling back until I land on my backside. I cry out as a sharp pain shoots up my spine. I forget the pain in an instant, though, when I lay my eyes on Dimitri. His fist is raised, but it's not in anger. He's . . . oh God . . .

He's scared.

The minute he realizes what he's done, his fist lowers and his face goes back to that mask he wears so well. But it's too late. I saw it. I saw the fear in his eyes. For a brief second, he thought I was someone else and when I laid my hand on him, it did something to him. He was frightened. Whatever happened to Dimitri, it was bad. It was bad enough that he can't stand to be touched, and it's not out of repulsion or memories, it's out of pure fear.

It hurts him in the depths of his soul to be touched without permission.

"I . . ." he begins, his voice thick with emotion. "I'm sorry."

I shake my head, putting my hands down by my sides and pushing myself up. I get to my feet, but I keep a good distance between us.

"It's my fault, I shouldn't have snuck up on you."

We stare, so much passing between us.

"How did you do it?"

I shake my head, confused. "Do what?"

"Move past the hatred."

I smile, but it's pathetic and weak. "I didn't move past it, Dimitri. I just learned how to keep it from consuming me."

He drops his eyes and then turns and stares back at the ocean. "I can't do that."

"Because you don't believe you can."

His body stiffens and he turns. "I'm tired. We're docking tomorrow at an island. I suggest you get rest."

Then he turns and leaves me.

Is the thought of facing all of this really that hard for him?

~

Oh.

Wow.

The island we're on is stunning. No, that doesn't even cover it. I've been on a few islands with Hendrix but this one . . . it outdoes them all. The sand isn't yellow, it's white. A fine, soft white that almost hurts your eyes to look at if the sun is facing in the right direction. The waves crashing against it are a crystal clear blue, so much so I can see everything that's beneath the water.

The trees are tall and green, surrounded by tiny shrubs that seem to be hugging each of them. There's a long, thin stream running from one end of the island to the other. I know, because I went for a walk the moment we got here. On the far-east end, there are some massive cliffs. I'm not about to go near them alone.

We've set up camp in a small clearing, using the trees to pitch our tents. It's getting to be quite cool of an evening, so we need shelter more than anything. Of course, we have the ship if all else fails, though I imagine, like me, nobody wants to be on the ship when they've got this paradise to be on. It's places like these that stop us from going crazy after weeks out on the water.

The pirate life is hard, but there are times it's also free. A big part of me will always belong to the ocean, to the freedom, to the family I created, but the other part of me desperately seeks life on the land. A life where I can just be me. But I have no doubt that if that day were to come, I'd miss the ocean. It would be hard not to.

"Where's Dimi?" Livvie asks, stopping beside me.

I'm sitting on the edge of the stream letting my feet run through the water. The moment I hear her voice, I sigh. She's a bratty, annoying woman, and there is absolutely no reason I can see that Dimitri could find anything about her interesting. Except maybe her boobs.

"How am I supposed to know?" I mutter.

"He's been gone for hours."

"And?"

"Well, you're always following him around."

I roll my eyes. I'm not getting into this with her. I know what she's doing and I'm not going to play that game.

"Well, I'm not with him so go and find him yourself."

She huffs and walks off. I sigh in pure relief. Three seconds with that girl has me wanting to stab my own eye with whatever blunt instrument I can find. I turn my focus back on the cool water when I hear shuffling beside me. I look over my shoulder to see Luke. God, I just can't escape.

"Where is Dimitri?"

"What the hell am I? An information center?"

He raises a brow, shaking his head.

"I don't know!" I cry, throwing my hands up. "I haven't seen him."

"He's been gone for hours, no one can find him."

I stand, growling. "I'll go find him, because it seems awfully clear to me none of you are going to do it."

"I just thought you might know. I'm not going to look for him."

I shake my head with a loud, exasperated sigh. "Why ask then?"

"I told you," he says simply. "I thought you might know."

I shake my head, stomping off into the thick, damp trees.

"Where are you going?" he yells.

"To find your boss."

"He probably doesn't want to be found."

"Too fucking bad," I mumble under my breath.

～

I begin to panic when I've been searching for two hours and there's no Dimitri. Granted, he could be back at camp and calling a search to find me now, but I can't risk that. I've reached the cliffs, after searching everywhere else for him. The sun is going to set in a matter of hours and it's getting cold. I take a deep breath and steel myself before climbing up and over the rocks.

I press my hand over my eyes to shield them from the sun so I can get a better view. Then I see him. He's sitting on a rock, head dropped, leg raised on a rock beside his foot. I'd say he was just sulking until I see that he's got blood on his leg. He's hurt. Without giving it a second thought, I rush toward him. It takes me a solid ten minutes because of all the rocks.

"Dimitri?" I say when I reach him.

He turns and looks at me; he looks shocked for a second. Like he expected someone else.

"Didn't think you'd be the one to show up," he mutters.

I knew I should have been a mind-reader.

"Everyone else was going to let you have space—aren't you lucky I'm smart enough to ignore them?"

His pained blue eyes meet mine, and he reminds me of a broken, sore puppy. He looks so . . . God, so depressed. I kneel down beside him and stare down at his leg. He's got a deep gash that's still bleeding quite well. His ankle is bruising too.

"What happened?"

"Slipped."

"Well, thanks for the detailed explanation. Can you walk?"

He looks sharply at me. "Would I be sitting here if I could walk?"

"All right, smart ass," I say, my voice sarcastic. "If you want my help, you better stop being so rude or I'll leave you here."

He doesn't answer for a second.

"What the hell is someone your size going to do?"

I stand and put my hands on my hips. "I'll have you know I'm quite explosive. I might be tiny, but boy do I bang—"

His lips twitch and when I realize how my words sound, I flush.

"I mean, go off with a bang."

That wasn't any better.

Now he's nearly smiling at me. God. So beautiful.

"Wh-whatever," I stammer. "Are you going to let me help you or not?"

"We'll never get back to the camp in time," he points out.

"Maybe, but sitting up here is stupid. You'll freeze."

He stares at me again. "What's your plan?"

I tilt my head, shocked that he's actually going to let me help him.

"Well, firstly, I have to put something on that gash. Which means you're going to have to let me touch you."

His body stiffens. "Hurry it up," he manages to grind out.

I nod and think about the best thing I can put on his leg. He needs to stop the bleeding. I stare at what he's wearing. Jeans, boots—well, one boot now—and a tight black T-shirt. I'd love to tell him to take that T-shirt off but I'm wearing something far more logical. A long—ish—dress. I lean down and press my fingers around on the ground until I find a sharp rock, then I shove it into my dress, tearing it. Once I have a small tear, I use both of my hands to rip a strip off.

It doesn't quite go as planned. Granted, I strip, but I also take half of my dress with it. I realize my panties are showing, and so are my horrible lily white legs. Great. I feel my cheeks go pink and I refuse to look at Dimitri as I kneel. Before I touch him, I look up. He's staring at me with that look again. That gorgeous, lusty, intense look.

"I know it doesn't mean anything and it won't change that this will be uncomfortable for you, but I need you to know I would never hurt you, Dimitri. Never."

His eyes soften and he narrows them, staring at me as though he just can't figure me out. I give him a weak smile and reach down, gently taking his ankle. He flinches and when I take a moment to peek at him, his jaw is tight and his eyes are closed. Poor man. I focus back on what I'm doing. I fasten the thickest part over the gash and then tie it tightly. When I'm done, I pat his knee softly and he opens his eyes.

"All done. You did good."

I stand and stare around, needing one more thing. I see a group of thick branches that have fallen from a tree nearby. I climb a few rocks until I reach them. I sort through them until I find a thick enough one that Dimitri can use to lean on as he walks. I take it back to him, and hold it out.

"It's now or never, soldier."

Oh, his eyes are all light and gorgeous again.

"What is the stick for?"

"Hate to break it to ya," I say casually, leaning on it. "But you're going to have to let me help you walk back. This is going to assist in our mission."

He quirks a brow. "Go on . . ."

"You'll hold the stick, see?" I say, demonstrating. "While your arm is around my shoulder. Together, the stick and I will help you back."

He's already shaking his head. "No, I'm six foot of muscle and you're . . ."

"What?" I challenge.

"You're tiny."

"Remember what I said about explosives?"

He shakes his head. "The stick will be fine."

"No," I say, holding it away from him when he reaches for it. "It won't be."

"Jessica, give me the stick."

"I shall not."

He drops his head and grumbles something before lifting it and trying again. "Give. Me. The. Stick."

"Do you want to die, Dimitri?"

"That's a stupid question."

I shake my head, twirling the stick with my fingertip. "No, it's quite logical given that you could get an infection, or make it worse by leaning on it, so, I ask again, do you want to die?"

"What do you think?"

"Well, from what I've guessed, no. But you never know. Being that you're all 'doom and gloom, must seek revenge' . . . and all that."

He rolls his eyes. "Do you ever stop talking?"

"Are you going to answer my question?"

"No," he grinds out. "I don't want to die."

"Good-O, then stand up and let me help you. If you don't, you'll stay up here and freeze or bleed to death. It's up to you."

He glares at me for a solid minute, but he does get to his feet. He's got his sore ankle off the ground, so I step forward and hand him the stick. He uses it to support his weight and I step closer, nudging my shoulder into his side.

"You can do it," I say in my best encouraging voice. It may or may not be a little sarcastic, too.

With an annoyed sigh, he lifts his arm and puts it over my shoulder.

"See, that wasn't so bad. I'm not buckling under your man muscles."

He sighs again.

"Come on then, we need to get off the rocks. To do that we need to navigate one at a time."

"Well, I wasn't about to leap over all of them. Fuck, you only gave me one stick. I might be good but shit . . ."

I feign a gasp. "Why, Dimitri. Was that a . . . dare I say . . . a joke?"

"Just keep walking."

"You and I will be great friends. Just you wait."

"Jessica," he says, his voice slightly amused.

"Yes?"

"Shut up."

"On it."

We manage to get over the rocks, figuring out if he sits on his bum and slides we can navigate them far easier. When we reach the flat ground, we can only move slowly. His ankle is hurting him—I can tell because he hisses every now and then, and I know it's not because of me, because I'm not talking to him. We reach the stream, but I know as well as he does that we've still got a solid hour and a half of walking left, and he's buckling already. The evening is about to be upon us and I don't know how much further I can push him.

"Stop here," I say, pointing to the stream. "Put your ankle in. Trust me, it'll feel better."

He doesn't argue. Pretty sure he knows I'm right. We sit beside the water and I help him put his foot in. I can see the instant relief on his face. I sit beside him, putting my sore feet in.

"I know I'm pretty super, but I'm not sure we'll make it back tonight. Any plans?"

"Are you always making jokes?" he asks randomly.

"Huh?" I say, giving him a puzzled expression.

"You seem to be able to find the funny in everything. Aside from the first night I tied you up, I've not seen genuine fear from you."

I shrug. "I've lived so long just doing as I needed to survive, I've never really had a chance to discover who 'Jess-slash-Blair' really is."

"How many people have seen this side to you?"

"That would be . . . one. You."

He turns to me, raising his brows. "Why?"

"I just told you why. When Hendrix first saved me, I was all kinds of fucked up. He helped me channel that until it got easier. Then I resigned myself to the fact that my life would forever be on that ship. I'd never love, I'd never marry, I'd never have kids. I just *was*. I kept to myself and I was thankful every day that he helped me survive. I wasn't afraid of you, despite your best attempts. And they were good attempts, by the way."

He smiles.

Oh God. He smiled.

My heart melts and my belly turns to a mass of liquid mess.

I force myself to keep talking, though my voice is wobbly. "I guess this is what's underneath it all. Underneath the broken girl and the girl who resigned herself to a life on the ship. I guess, really, when all the skin is stripped back, this is Blair. Jess is quiet, Jess does as she's told, Jess is broken and is too damned scared to let herself feel. Blair, she's different. She's the beauty before the pain. She's the witty, funny girl that I have no doubt I would have grown to be if given the chance."

"You're Blair," he says, his voice deep and throaty. "The girl I see, she's Blair."

I smile at him, the first real smile I've given for so many years I can't count.

"And who are you, Dimitri?"

He turns and stares at me, his eyes hard. "I'm Dimitri."

"Okay, I will rephrase. Who is this?" I point to his chest. "Right here, right now."

He looks away. "We need to find somewhere to sleep."

"Are you always going to avoid my questions?"

He shrugs. "I don't have to answer them."

"No," I mutter. "I suppose you don't. Fine, have it your way. Where can we sleep?"

He looks around and it's slowly beginning to get dark. He points to a small overhanging rock. "That'll have to do."

I help him up and we walk over. There's just enough room under the rock for one body. Nice.

"You sleep under it, I'll be fine just leaning against it," he says.

"Whatever you want."

We both sit down under it for now and stare out at the sun setting.

"It's a beautiful island."

"It's my peace," he admits.

"I can see why."

"I have a question for Jess . . ."

I turn to him. "She's listening."

He hesitates for a moment.

"What happens under this rock stays under this rock, Dimi."

He shoots me a look. "Why did you call me that?"

"I think it's who you are now. Dimi. Your Dimitri is like my Blair. Very few see the real you. So, you're just like my Jess right now. Dimi is the other side of you, the side you've created for yourself."

He shakes his head, not bothering to argue. "Was there ever a time you wanted to make him pay?"

I turn to him, meeting his gaze. "I did make him pay, Dimi. I killed him."

He tilts his head. "Was it worth it in the end? Was it what healed you?"

"I'm not healed," I say, turning away. "I'm surviving. There's a massive difference. Each night I sleep, I still see his disfigured body. The years don't take that away, they only blur it. It's like a TV you can hear but can't see. But to answer your question, no, it wasn't worth it in the end."

"Why not?"

I shake my head, swallowing. "Because it made me a murderer. It made me into something I don't like living with. It changed me from a victim to someone who became exactly the same. I took a life. Justified or not, it wasn't my life to take. So no, it wasn't worth it. Did I want him to suffer? Yes. But a life is a life all the same, and taking one hurts no matter the reason you take it."

He's silent for a long while. When I turn to look at him, he's staring at the setting sun. A cool breeze comes in, tickling my face and making me shiver.

"It's going to be a cold night and you're wearing half a dress," Dimitri finally says. "Take my shirt."

"You'll freeze. It might be half a dress but at least the top half is long."

I stare down at the cream and brown dress I'm wearing. I'm thankful right now it's got long sleeves.

"Jess, don't argue."

I raise my brows at him. "You'll freeze. We'll be fine. I'm fine."

He shakes his head. "Women."

"That wasn't very nice."

He doesn't answer me and we sit in silence as the sun goes down.

I won't admit I'm kind of happy to feel him so close to me.

But I'm also scared—God only knows what's out here at night.

CHAPTER FOURTEEN

Jess

It's freezing.

No, that doesn't even cover it. The word freezing just doesn't do it.

My teeth are clattering together and my entire body is shaking so hard I feel as though I'm convulsing. I can feel Dimitri beside me, but not close enough that I have the privilege of gathering body heat.

"Jesus," he mumbles. "It's cold. Are you okay?"

"I-I-I-I." I can't even speak, great.

He rolls and sits up, reaching out. I feel his hand touch my face. It's warm. How the hell is it warm?

"You're fucking freezing."

"I-I-I-I . . ."

"Shit," he grumbles.

He's still for a moment before letting out a deep sigh and saying, "Move out for a second."

I do as he says, moving out from the hanging rock. He shuffles around and then says, "Come back."

I go to get back in only to smash into his hard chest. "W-w-w-w-what?"

"I don't want to die. You don't want to die. Body heat."

Logical.

I don't argue. I'm too cold.

"Just . . . don't touch me."

Seriously?

"A-a-a-a-are you s-s-s-s-serious?"

"Lie beside me, I'll wrap you up but don't . . . don't touch me."

Fine. Whatever.

I lie down beside him and he pulls me into his arms, doing just as he said. Wrapping me up. He curls himself around me and I feel his body heat pouring into me. Oh. Yes. Thank God. After about ten minutes, I finally begin to feel my fingers and toes again—but sleep is not happening.

"I can't sleep," I say, shifting to make sure I don't "touch" him.

"That's probably because we're on the ground, and it's hard."

"Probably. Want to play a game?"

He makes a rumbling sound with his chest. "I don't play games."

"Don't be such a fun spoiler."

He sighs. "Dare I ask what the game is?"

"Okay, so we'll ask one question each about each other. We have to answer it, even if we don't want to."

"Not happening," he says firmly.

"Okay, unless it's a really painful question to answer."

"Still not happening."

"I'll go first, ask me something."

He hesitates for a minute or two, but finally says, "Has there been anyone else since . . . him?"

I shake my head and I know he can feel it. "Not one person."

He goes silent; it seems to be what he does when he has nothing to say about a situation. Well, I guess most of us are silent if we have nothing to say.

"My turn," I say softly. "I've taken a good guess and I imagine you sleep around quite a bit. Correct me if I'm wrong, of course. But, if I'm right—why all the women?"

He shrugs. "I'm a man."

"That's such a man answer!"

He chuckles—oh that sound.

"They just make me feel better for a moment or two. It helps."

"I wish I had that," I admit. "The very idea of sex scares me so badly I've never wanted to try it. But then, I've never had anyone I trust enough to try it with."

"What about your beloved Hendrix?"

"Hendrix and I were never like that. He always, *always* respected me."

No answer again.

"But I guess for you, with women like Livvie around, you don't have to think too much about what you're getting."

He snorts. "Livvie is . . ."

He pauses, weighing up his answer.

"Is easy. Is gorgeous. Is what every man would pick. I mean, why wouldn't they? Girls like me, we don't compare to someone like her."

"It's hard to compare average and perfect."

"Fuck, ouch, Dimi!"

He shakes his head. I feel his cheek press against my head as he does. "She's average, Jess."

Oh.

My cheeks flush.

"Livvie is a basic idea of what women think men want. Yes, she's gorgeous, yes she's easy, but that's as far as it goes. She's the same as a thousand other women. She's fake all over. Women like you, they're different. You're not the same as a thousand others, you're one of your own. So while you might not be the stereotype, you can be so much more beautiful."

Oh. My. God.

My mouth drops open and I struggle to take a breath of fresh air. Did he just . . . did he . . . call me beautiful?

"My hair is red," I manage to stammer out.

"It's fucking gorgeous."

"My skin . . . is so white."

"Like a doll."

"My eyes are too big."

"The bigger, the better."

"Stop it!" I cry. "Why are you being so nice to me? Is it because you know I could leave you out here?"

He falls silent. "I may be a whole lot of things, Jess, but I'm not a liar."

"So you're just being honest with me?"

"Something like that."

Damn, pin to the ego bubble. I push from his arms. "I need air."

"You're in the open . . ." he points out.

I get up anyway, regretting the decision immediately. It's freezing and the warmth I just managed to get into my body is now rushing out and being replaced with a bone-chilling cold. I wrap my arms around myself and inhale. In and out. In and out. Just focus.

"Get back in here, you'll freeze," Dimi yells.

"Did you know I've never been kissed?"

It's such a stupid thing to say, yet the need to say it seems to far outweigh logic.

"What?" he mutters, his voice laced with confusion.

"He raped me, he took so much from me, but he never kissed me. He never stole that from me. Since then, I never took it from anyone. I just . . . let it be. When I get kissed, I want it to be because both he and I want it. It needs to be slow, and powerful, and everything a first kiss should be." I stop and take a deep, shaky breath, gathering myself and pushing aside my emotion. "My dreams of falling in love and getting married, living happily ever after were stripped of me when he took my innocence. The one dream I was left with was that maybe someday I'd have that life-stopping kiss."

"Why are you telling me?"

I sigh, shaking my head. "Well, Dimi, you're the first person I've ever, in my entire life, thought about giving it to."

Silence.

Long, agonizing silence.

"You don't want to give me something like that, Jess. I'm far from worthy."

"Whose opinion is that?" I whisper.

"It's mine."

"And it's not mine."

"Get back in here," he says, his voice tired. "We need to rest."

"I'm not comfortable with that close proximity when I just confessed that I'd like you to kiss me."

He's quiet again.

"Just get in."

"Bossy," I mutter, kneeling down and crawling back in.

The minute I'm in, he pulls me back to the position we were in before. The moment the warmth fills me again, I sigh. Thank God, I needed this. So badly. I yawn and feel my eyes getting heavy. I feel bad for Dimitri sleeping on the hard, cold ground. I can tell by his breathing that he's not settling down—his heart is pounding against my cheek and his chest is rising and falling heavily.

"What's on your mind that has you breathing like that?" I whisper, yawning again.

"Kissing you."

My yawn halts and I snap my mouth closed. Kissing . . . me? He's thinking about kissing me? Oh.

"Is that a good thought or a bad thought?"

His chest shakes with suppressed laughter. "Usually good."

My cheeks grow hot and my heart begins to pound. I've not for one second since I was a young girl thought about kissing a man. I've never wanted it. I've never tried to get it. I honestly started to believe that I would end up alone, cold, and never wanting it. I thought maybe he'd taken my desire away along with my innocence.

We're both silent. The only sounds between us are the sounds of the night creatures, singing and shuffling, and our own deep, ragged breaths. I swallow over and over, trying to take my mind off the thought of kissing Dimitri. My heart is pounding so heavily it actually hurts. As if someone above thought it would be funny to play a joke on me, my stomach decides to drop one hell of a cramp.

Really, God? You choose now to drop that on me?

I groan and shift, trying to get comfortable. It doesn't help that I'm left with little protection out here. Damn you, Aunt Flo, you're always picking the worst moments to show your face.

"You okay?" Dimitri asks.

"I just . . . I have a cramp."

"Want to shift?"

"Not . . . that kind of cramp."

"Oh," he says, shifting about. Clearly that made him uncomfortable.

"I need to move again, just for a second."

He lets his arms go from around me, and I crawl out of the warmth and stand. I put my hands out in front of me and find the nearest tree. I have one tampon stashed in my pocket to get me by until morning and I am thinking now is the best time to use it. I quickly change it, stumbling a few times and cursing as I dig a big enough hole to hide the other one. It's really the worst possible thing I could have right now. My cheeks are flushing with shame.

"What are you doing?" Dimitri yells. "Killing an animal?"

"Very funny," I mutter, dusting my hands off. I don't even want to know how dirty I'll be by morning.

I navigate my way back to Dimitri and I crawl back into his arms. He takes me in easily, not hesitating when I put my head back on his chest. I try to get comfortable but it seems like that's not likely with the pain radiating through my lower belly and down my legs. I get bad cramps; it's always been something I've struggled with. I whimper and shift.

"They're bad, aren't they?" Dimitri asks.

"Yes. It's okay, they'll go eventually."

He moves me so I'm on my side and his hand slides down, taking hold of the hem of my dress.

"Whoa, what are you doing?" I cry, pulling away from him.

"Warmth helps," he murmurs, sliding his hand under my dress and finding the soft spot between my hips. Thank God it's high enough that he's not anywhere near my womanly bits. But he manages to find the exact spot I'm cramping. He puts a small amount of pressure on my belly by pressing down, and the warmth of his hand does seem to help.

"It'll get better the longer my hand is here."

"Thank you," I whisper.

"Now, try to sleep."

I feel my eyes drooping and I know sleep is something I really need to concentrate on. I'm exhausted and so is he. I close my eyes, breathing in and out deeply, inhaling his warm, manly scent. I find my body dropping off quickly and when the warmth from his hand finally penetrates, easing my cramping, I drift off to sleep.

"Goodnight, Blair," I think I hear him murmur before the world goes dark.

CHAPTER FIFTEEN

Jess

Morning comes quickly after we finally drift off. I wake because the sun is burning into my eyelids, making it feel as though I'm lying directly under it. I groan and stretch. Dimitri is wrapped around me, his hard body pressed against mine. There's a massive amount of heat between us and the moment I shift out of his arms, it escapes, letting me feel the cool breeze outside.

I get to my knees, looking down at Dimitri.

He's half on his side, half on his back. His dark hair is messy, and there are twigs poking out from the thick depths. His skin is dirty and he looks like he's done two rounds with a puddle of mud yet he looks so utterly perfect my breath catches in my throat. I manage to compose myself enough to steady my breathing. I focus on inhaling the fresh morning breeze.

I walk over to the stream and kneel down, my knees burning as small rocks poke into my skin. I shift and groan, cupping my hands and placing them into the water. I splash my face and then turn my attention to washing my arms and trying to remove some of the dirt I've managed to accumulate through the night.

"You're crazy."

I turn and see Dimitri staring down at me. He's shirtless and he's got a hand up in his hair, tugging the thick strands, trying to tidy them up.

"It's a good way to wake up," I say, splashing my face again.

"It's fucking cold."

"Yes, yes it is."

He kneels beside me and dunks his shirt in. He lifts it, wrings it out and presses it against his face. He shudders and makes a horrified sound, then turns to me with a wide-eyed expression.

"I'll say it again, you're crazy."

I shrug and get to my feet. "Crazy and starving. Are you ready to get going?"

He nods and throws his shirt over his shoulder. I stare down at his ankle—it's far less swollen and he seems to be able to put pressure on it, so that's a good thing.

"How's your leg?"

He stares down at it and shrugs again. "The bleeding has stopped on the gash and my ankle feels a lot better."

"Good. Do you need your stick?" I ask, nodding toward the tree where he laid it.

"Yeah, can't hurt."

He walks over and takes it, and we head back to the camp.

~

"Talk about fuckin' scare us!" Luke mutters, shoving Dimitri in the shoulder.

"Sorry. We didn't want to risk walking at night and my ankle was killing me."

I give the group a brief smile and then turn and head toward the ship. They've been all over Dimi since we got back, making sure he's okay. For a moment, just a small second, this group reminded me of Hendrix and the pirates. My heart aches to know if they're okay, but there's no way for me to do that. I just have to hang in there until a plan becomes more clear.

I do know one thing, though.

I can't kill Dimi.

Part of me wanted to, thinking it was truly the only way I could save Hendrix, but now I've learned a little more about him—I realize I just can't do it. Dimitri isn't bad at heart. Hell, he's not even really bad anywhere else either. He's just looking for a way to bring himself peace. I can't judge him for that. I've been in that position before. Even if it was for just a little while, I've still been there.

"Hey, Jess."

I turn at the sound of Dimi's voice. His eyes meet mine and I can see genuine gratitude in their depths.

"Thank you."

I give him a weak smile and nod, then I turn and continue on my way back to the ship.

Something doesn't feel right in my belly, and I'm not sure what it is.

~

Dimitri

"I can't find him. We've been out here two weeks and I've let out every fucking radar we have and he hasn't come," I mutter, pacing up and down the sand two days after we docked at the island.

"I don't know, boss," Luke says, putting his hands on his hips and leaning against a tall palm tree.

"He's up to something. He's smarter than I thought. I was expecting him to go to any lengths to get Jess back, but he's not. He's making us wait, he's making us think he's forgotten about her. Luckily for me, I know that's not the case."

She isn't easy to forget.

I shake her from my head. I shake the memories of her curled in my arms all night and the fact that I didn't feel sick being so close to her. I shake the feelings that are swelling in my chest. She can't mean anything to me, it's not how this plan was meant to unfold.

"Maybe something has happened to him?" Luke suggests, snapping me back to reality.

I shake my head. "No, he's too smart for that. He's working something. I'm just not sure what it is."

"Well, there are definitely other ships out there. Marco picked some up this morning, southwest, about a hundred miles."

I nod. "We're spending only one more night here. Chances are they're just carrier ships, but I am not naive enough to think we're the only criminals on this ocean. Hendrix ain't the only one either."

"More pirates?"

"Yeah, more pirates."

He nods and pulls out a cigarette. "See Linden got a boar this morning? Having a cookout tonight."

"Yeah," I say, staring out at the ocean.

Jess is sitting on the sand, smiling out at the sea, a look of complete calm on her face.

Stop looking, Dimitri.

Don't let her affect you.

Fuck, it's too late. She already is.

~

Hendrix hasn't come for me.

I overheard Dimitri, even though he thought I couldn't hear him. When there's no other noise around, it's not hard to hear what's going on around you. I heard bits and pieces of what Dimi said, and from what I can gather, Hendrix hasn't jumped into his trap like he wanted. That surprises me—Hendrix is a hothead sometimes and I honestly thought he would have run off the rails and dived in.

He didn't.

That could be because of Indi. She would be holding him back, keeping him on level ground so he doesn't act without thinking. She's good like that. It could also be because Hendrix is smarter than I first thought. I actually feel bad that for a second there, I doubted him. He's a pirate; he's been running these waters for years. He knows them better than anyone else.

He wouldn't just let Dimitri destroy everything he's built so easily. The feeling of intense relief I feel in my chest is comforting. I've struggled with the thought that I might never make it home, but now that I know there's still a chance and that Hendrix is probably coming up with a sturdy plan, I'm far more confident.

I sigh and drop back into the water. The waves that crash along the shoreline are calming, almost like a drug. I sigh once more, only this time it's longer and drawn out. I tilt my head back into the water and let the cool ease my aching neck. I'm still stiff and sore from sleeping on the ground with Dimitri.

"We're having a fire."

I lift my head and see Dimitri standing on the sand, only his ankles in the water. I can't help but smile at the image. He's gorgeous—no, scrap that, he's a breath of fresh air. A god. A mold that was broken and never created again.

"Hello?" he says.

I blink. Shit, I was staring.

"I . . . sorry. A fire, you said?"

He gives me a lazy half-smile that has me clenching my thighs together.

"Yeah, you know, the burny orange thing that people use to cook on."

"Ha ha," I smile, standing and walking out of the waves. "I know what a fire is."

"Really?" he says, following me as I walk up the beach. I can hear the sarcasm in his voice.

"Really, really."

"How are the cramps going?"

I smile but I keep my voice steady so he doesn't know I'm smiling.

"Dimi?"

"What?"

"It's never okay to ask a woman about her period."

He's quiet for a moment, I can only hear his footsteps as he follows closely behind me.

"You women are completely confusing."

"Yes, yes we are."

"You want help when you're hurtin', but you don't want us to 'ask' about it."

"Okay, let me put it like this—you know when a woman has a period, you know when she's cramping, but you never, I repeat *never* ask her directly about it."

"Jesus," he mutters.

"Precisely."

We reach the camp and I can see everyone sitting around a large, beautiful fire. I smile, my body shivering with need as we draw closer. A fire brings a certain level of peace. It's warm and you can just sit staring at it for hours, not thinking, not feeling, just enjoying. I realize I'm smiling stupidly when Livvie clears her throat. I turn my gaze in her direction to see her glaring at me.

"Dimi," she sings. "Come sit by me. I'm cold."

"There's a fire," he points out, but he still walks toward her.

My chest clenches—with jealousy or just frustration, I don't know. I take a seat on a long, thick log beside Luke. He's sitting with a young crew member. I've not noticed him before, but that's probably because I've been wrapped very tightly in Dimitri's grasp. I stare at the man and when he notices, he smiles at me. I can't help but smile back—he has a kind face.

He's got big brown eyes and dark brown hair. His skin is olive and his body is tall and muscular. He's a very good-looking man. I really don't know how I missed him. In fact, the more I look around this group, the more I realize I've not taken any notice of any of them. I feel like an ass now, they must think I'm a complete bitch.

"Hi," Brown Eyes smiles.

"Hey," I smile back. "I'm Jess."

"I know," he grins.

"And you are?" I prompt.

"Zed."

"That's a cool name."

He reaches down, lifting a bottle of rum. He pushes it toward me. "It is. Want a drink?"

"Is that all you boys drink? Rum?" I tease. "Sure you're not pirates?"

Zed laughs. "I'm pretty sure we're pretend pirates, does that count?"

I take the bottle and take a long sip. It burns as it goes down, but it's a great relief.

"It counts to me. Know any good jokes?"

He laughs, shaking his head. "I haven't taken Pirate Jokes 101, sorry."

"Me either, it's on my TDL."

He raises his brows. "TDL?"

"To do list."

He shakes his head and I beam.

"So how come I haven't spoken to you or seen you around?"

He shrugs. "Probably because you were under the boss's wing. That and I'm working a lot of the time."

"Working?"

"I navigate."

"Ah," I say, nodding. "You make sure we don't get lost."

He chuckles. "That amongst other things."

"Like?"

"Like tracking."

I frown. "Right."

"Sorry," he murmurs, looking genuinely sympathetic that he's been hired to track the man who saved my life.

"No problem," I manage through gritted teeth.

"Come on," he says, pushing the bottle back toward me. "I'm only doin' my job. Don't judge me for that."

He's giving me the eyes—the pleading puppy dog eyes. I giggle and shake my head, rolling my eyes. "God, fine, okay. Give me that."

I take the bottle and have a drink, feeling for the first time in weeks like things might just go how they're meant to.

And surprisingly, I feel content.

CHAPTER SIXTEEN

Jess

L ouder, louder!" I giggle, spinning around in a circle.

I'm drunk—no, I'm beyond drunk. I've gone to the level of crazy and I'm rocking it. I've been dancing to my own voice for the past half an hour, singing and spinning until I land in a heap on the sand, then I start again. I have most of the guys in fits of laughter; I've even seen Dimi smiling here and there. His eyes haven't left me, though, even when Malibu Barbie tried to crawl onto his lap.

"Zed!" I yell. "Sing louder."

Zed has joined in now and we've skipped off to the sand. He's now perched on a rock singing "Cotton Eye Joe" to me in his best country voice. It's not very good but I'm not about to break that to him. He sings louder and I spin harder, twirling until my stomach turns. I drop onto the sand with a loud laugh. Zed leaps off the rock and runs over, plonking down beside me.

"Ever tried to make shapes out of the stars?" I giggle, staring up at the small stars streaking across the sky.

"No."

"Try," I encourage, squinting to see through the haze. Nope, I'm too drunk to see them clearly.

"You go first."

"Okay," I say, concentrating. I let my blurred vision slide over the stars until I'm sure I can see a shape. "Oh, look, that one looks like a penis."

Zed snorts and chuckles. "Seriously?"

"Yeah, look, there."

I point up to the sky.

"Yep, there's about a billion stars up there."

"Look harder," I urge. "It's right there, pointing to the moon."

Zed bursts out laughing. "Are you serious?"

"Serious," I cry, wiggling my legs. "Look."

"Zed?"

I hear Dimitri's voice and I turn to see him standing in the sand, arms crossed, looking down at us. Zed leaps up, dusting the sand off his jeans. "Sorry, boss, just lookin' at stars."

"I got it from here. Go and finish up with the guys."

He nods and flashes me a smile. "Later, Jess."

"Later, Zed, thanks for making a penis with me."

He chuckles and shakes his head, disappearing into the trees. Dimitri takes his spot, lying beside me. He puts his hands up behind his head. My body becomes aware of his presence and in my drunken state, I'm finding it very hard not to roll toward him.

"Do I even want to know what you two were doing?"

I giggle. "We were making shapes out of the stars. I saw a penis—he couldn't see it."

Dimitri turns to me, raising his brows. "Pretty sure there's no penis shapes up there."

"There's a penis, Dimi. Don't you doubt it."

He laughs softly. "It's getting cold, you should go and get some rest. It's nearly two a.m."

I raise my brows, rolling clumsily onto my side. "Seriously?"

"Yep."

"Let's go for a swim first."

"Not sure that's wise."

I pout. "What did I say about being a fun-spoiler? Come on."

I get up after a few hilarious attempts, and I stumble forward toward the ocean.

"Whoa there," Dimitri says, wrapping an arm around my waist and hauling me backwards. "You'll kill yourself."

I huff. "No I won't, it's fine."

"Come on, you're drunk and you need to sleep."

"But, Dimi," I whine. "I want to swim."

He makes an amused sound and pulls me toward the ship that's docked on the sand. He helps me up the ladder, which ends in a lot of giggles and curse words from him. By the time we get halfway to his room, he's given up and has scooped down and lifted me into his arms.

"I can walk," I protest, attempting to squirm. It's really useless. He's too strong.

"I have no doubt, but it's far quicker this way."

"Can we go for a swim?"

"No."

"Please, Dimi."

He smiles and I reach up and touch his cheek where a lone dimple appears. "You have only one dimple."

"Is that right?"

I nod, poking it with my finger. "That's right. Do you think it's a deformity?"

"You're a sweetheart, really . . ."

I giggle. "I'm not insulting you, Dimi. I think it's cute."

"Well, now you're insulting me."

"Why?" I ask, now stroking the stubble on his cheeks.

"Because you just called me cute."

A giggle bubbles up in my throat, but I smother it.

"What's wrong with cute?"

108

"Cute is what you call the guy you don't think is good-looking, but you don't want to insult."

I laugh, shaking my head and poking his bottom lip with my finger. "Okay, how about this? You're sexy, hot, smokin', panty-melter, the wetter of all pussies everywhere."

He laughs loudly. "Are you fuckin' serious?"

"People are asking me that a lot tonight," I frown. "And yes, I'm serious. There are many women with uncomfortable vaginas right now because you gave them the sex eyes."

His chest is rumbling with laughter and it makes me smile. "Uncomfortable vaginas? Really?"

"It's a very serious issue, Dimi. Don't blow it off. One look from you and boom, we've got some serious leakage."

"Jesus, stop. You're making vaginas sound like they've got a condition."

I laugh loudly and poke him in the chest. "You're the one that gives them a condition."

He drops me onto his bed and stares down at me. "And how's your vagina?"

I give him a disgusted face. "That's such an ugly word, right?"

"What would you prefer your condition to be referred to as?"

I cross my arms. "I never said I had the condition."

He's giving me that half-smile again. Shit.

"You never said you didn't, either."

"Smartass. Your sex eyes don't work on me."

He lies down on the bed beside me. "Is that right?"

"It's very right."

"Okay then," he murmurs, yawning.

"If you're tired, you can sleep. I'm going swimming," I say, getting up and crawling to the end of the bed.

Dimitri launches up, catching me around the waist and pulling me down.

"No you ain't."

"Are you always so bossy?"

Boy, did I just slur? Not classy, Jess. Not classy at all.

"You need water, stay here."

He holds my chest down as he moves to get up. "Stay. Here."

I smile up at him, fluttering my lashes. "I'm not going anywhere."

"I don't believe you."

My grin is too sly. He turns and digs through his drawers, still holding me down. He reappears with a set of cuffs. He snaps them on my hands before I get a chance to pull away. Well, maybe I tried to pull away but, because of the level of intoxication I'm experiencing, I probably moved no faster than a turtle.

"That's cheating," I slur, feeling my eyes drop closed.

He doesn't say anything, he just leaves and comes back a moment later with a glass of water. He presses the cold glass to my cheek, causing my eyes to snap back open.

"Drink this before you pass out."

I mumble something and take the glass, drinking the entire thing in three gulps. I thrust it back at him and the minute he takes it out of my fingers, my hand flops down beside me. I yawn and my head spins as my eyes begin to drop closed again.

"Shift so I can put the blankets on you."

Dimitri moves me, but I don't open my eyes. Instead I continue mumbling incoherent words over and over. I feel his fingers stroke down my cheek once he's managed to get me tucked in.

Then I pass out.

CHAPTER SEVENTEEN

Dimitri

I feel her stir beside me and I groan, rolling onto my side. A hand touches my cheek, causing my eyes to pop open. Jess is staring down at me, and the faint light from the lamp only just outlines her face. Her fingers run down my cheek and stop at my lips. She's looking at them, like she wants to consume them. I feel my skin tingle.

"Dimi, I changed my mind," she mumbles, her voice still a little slurred.

Shit, she's not completely sober. Which means anything coming out of her mouth right now I'm going to pay little attention to.

"You should get some sleep."

She leans forward suddenly, plastering her lips against mine. I don't see it coming, therefore I don't react how I'm sure she wants me to. She's caught me off guard. Besides, this isn't how this is meant to go for her. She deserves her first kiss to be out of this world. I reach up, taking her shoulders. I push her back gently.

"No, Jess. I don't want . . ."

Her entire body stiffens and she jerks backwards, stumbling off the bed before I can finish my sentence. She's got her fingertips pressed to her lips and she's staring down at me with an expression filled with hurt and shame. No, fuck, no, I didn't mean her to think I didn't want it. I sit up, reaching across, but she turns and bolts into the bathroom, slamming the door loudly.

Fuck.

That didn't go as planned.

~

Jess

"Shit, fuck, Jess," I hear him say as I drop down beside the bathroom door.

I'm ashamed. I just woke him up and, without thinking, threw myself at him and kissed him. It was an awful kiss, too. Hard and rough. I'm almost sure I'm bleeding slightly from my bottom lip because I hit his face so forcefully. I rub my face, trying to hide my shame. He rejected me. All along I've been wanting him far more than he wanted me.

"Jess," he says, banging on the door. "Open up."

I can't sit here all night, but at the same time thinking about seeing him is far worse than this cold floor.

"Jess," he says again. "You read me wrong."

I don't see how.

I pull my knees up to my chest and put my face between them, taking a few deep breaths. I have to face him, but I'm afraid he'll see the shame I'm hiding there. I slowly shove to my feet and hesitate at the door. With another deep breath, I swing it open and face a gentle expression. He feels sorry for me. I can see it. That's just great. I need to go back to sleep and forget this ever happened.

"It's fine, Dimi," I say, shoving past him. "I had too much to drink. I wasn't thinking. I get it. You don't want me like that. I read it wrong. It's not your fault. It's—"

"Jesus, Jess, shut the fuck up."

I turn to him, gaping. "I beg your pardon?"

"Shut. The. Fuck. Up."

I cross my arms. "There's no need to be so mean."

He's smiling. Why is he smiling? He stalks toward me with an expression that has me taking two steps back. When he reaches me, his hand curls around the back of my neck and he pulls me so close I can feel his warm breath on my lips. I stop breathing.

"I didn't kiss you back because it wasn't how it was meant to go for you. You told me you wanted it to be amazing, something both parties felt. You waking up and jumping me isn't the way that was meant to go down. No, you should have a man pressing himself against you, making your breath halt in your throat."

I gasp. It's doing that.

He slides a finger down my cheek.

"It should make tingles break out on your skin."

My entire body prickles.

"It should make everything come alive, until you can think of nothing else but having that person's lips on yours."

I lick my bottom lip and I take a step closer, pressing my body to his.

"You wanted it to be memorable," he murmurs, staring at my lips. "I'm just making sure it is."

"Oh you a-a-a-are, are you?" I whisper.

"Yeah, baby, I am. Now, we can make this awesome or we can let you beat me up with your lips again."

"I'd like it to be awesome." I smile weakly.

"I think you've made the right choice. Brace yourself."

I'm still smiling when he closes in. It seems like it takes forever for his lips to finally touch mine, but when they do, fireworks explode. His lips are soft, wet, and so damned consuming. I feel the urge to press myself against him, taking as much as I can, feeling as much as possible. He groans, reaching up and taking hold of my hair, tugging my head backwards so he can deepen the kiss.

I've had a lot of fantasies about how a first kiss might feel— this outweighs all of those. The way Dimitri moves his lips over mine is causing my mind to spin. When he slides his tongue into my mouth and it dances with mine, my knees buckle. My hands raise to press against his chest, when I remember he doesn't like to be touched. Slowly, I lower them back to my sides. This seems to please him so much that he bends me back slightly, kissing me with everything he is.

By the time we pull apart, my body is throbbing and my lips are swollen. I press my fingertips to them and stare up into his eyes. "That was . . ."

He grins. "Worth all your fantasies?"

"More," I breathe. "So much more."

His eyes soften and crinkle at the sides as he smiles. "I'm glad."

"You are definitely up there in the top ten." I smile.

He chuckles. "Get some sleep."

We walk over to the bed and crawl back into it. I can feel him beside me even though he's not touching me.

"Dimi?"

"Mmmm."

"Thanks."

He's quiet for a long moment. "Anytime," he finally whispers.

CHAPTER EIGHTEEN

Jess

Take this, it has my number and Luke's in it. If you get lost in the crowd, you can call me. I'm taking it as soon as we're out of here, but you'll need it while we're in."

I stare down at the phone Dimi has just handed me as he pulls me along through the crowd. We're at another fight—he needed more information, though he won't tell me what about. I'm not happy about seeing him fight again, but there's no way he's letting me out of his sight now we're back on land again.

"Okay," I say as we reach the back door. He shoves it open and steps in.

There are more people in this back room than there were during the last fight we were at. There seem to be more fighters, too.

"I hate you fighting," I mumble as he pulls me to a locker.

"I know," he says, bumping his fist on the cool metal and busting it open. He pulls out a pair of boxing gloves.

"You box?"

He looks at me quickly before yanking his shirt off and strapping his hands before sliding the gloves on. "Yeah, I do a few different styles."

"Is this one you're good at?"

He grins, tilting his head back and bouncing from side to side. Here we go again.

"Don't stress, I won't get hurt."

"You can't know that."

"I can know that."

I shake my head, watching him bounce about like he's high.

"Rex is here, boss. He wants to speak with you," Luke says, coming up behind me.

"Send him in."

"Who's Rex?" I ask, sitting on a long bench.

"He has the information I need."

I nod and stare down at my feet, trying to control my nerves. I don't want to think too much about Dimi and the fight he's about to enter into. I certainly don't want to think about the "information" he's receiving.

"Dimitri, long time no see."

I lift my head to see a man walking into the room behind Luke. I can't see him fully because Luke is so big, but when he steps aside, everything in my world stops. My vision blurs and I sway in my seat. I can't be seeing it right. I can't be. He's dead. He's *dead*. I begin gasping for air as I manage to push myself up to my feet and step behind Dimitri. I reach out and take hold of his arms from behind, needing to be holding onto someone right now. He flinches at the contact.

It's him.

My foster father.

I don't know how he's still alive, I don't even know how he's here, but it's him. His face is . . . God . . . so fucked up. It's scarred so badly it would take a person who has known him for a long while to recognize him. One of his eyes is permanently closed; it looks like it's fused together. His skin is bumpy and damaged and his hair is now graying and wispy. He's as awful as he was back then.

Dimitri turns, his expression hard. That is, until he sees mine. I'm staring at Roger, my foster father, and I'm barely breathing. I killed him. I'm sure of it. There was so much blood, he wasn't breathing. At least, I thought he wasn't. I don't remember a great deal about that night. But . . . I was so sure . . . no . . . no, this can't be right. It can't be.

"Hey," Dimitri says. "Jess, look at me."

I lift my eyes, and I can feel my lip quivering. His eyes narrow and he jerks his glove off, reaching up and cupping my cheek. "What is it?"

"Dimitri?" Roger says, stepping closer. "I don't have long."

Dimitri turns and glares at him. "I need a minute, my girl is upset."

His girl.

My knees buckle from the mass of emotions running through me. It's not real. It's just someone who looks like him. He's dead, I remember it. I saw him bleed. I stabbed him so many times. He's dead, Jess. Dead. He's dead.

"Well, hurry it—" Roger begins. "You've got to be kidding me."

Dimitri mutters a curse and glares at Roger again, but Roger's gaze is on me. He's finally noticed me. I can't breathe. My knees tremble and I am still grasping Dimitri, not willing to let his arms go. Roger's evil blue eye is wide and horrified, but it quickly turns to anger.

"You fucking little slut!"

Dimitri spins around, shoulders back, expression livid.

"What the fuck did you just call her?"

"I've been lookin' for you for years, you little whore. Do you see what you did to me, Blair? I'm gonna fuckin' kill you."

He lunges toward me, and with a cry I scramble backwards. Dimitri steps in front of him, his fist lashing out and connecting with Roger's face. A loud crack fills the room and Roger's nose begins gushing blood down his face.

"Step back!" he roars.

Roger stops, throwing a hand up to his nose. He turns his angry glare to Dimitri. "I've got business with her. Step aside."

"You'll not go near her!"

Roger glares at me, his body stiff, but he steps back. "If it wasn't for the massive amount of money you're going to bring me, I'd put you on your ass, Dimitri."

"You need to get out of this fuckin' room, now."

"With pleasure," Roger growls, then his eye turns to mine. "We're not done, Blair."

He turns and leaves the room, and I fall to my knees. My entire body is trembling and I'm sobbing. Any wall I'd built up for myself is just crumbling into thousands of tiny pieces. Dimitri drops to his knees beside me and puts his hands on my shoulders.

"Jess, look at me."

I lift my eyes, but tears are streaming down my face.

"Who was that?"

My lip quivers as I open my mouth and rasp, "That was *him*, Dimi."

He doesn't need more of an explanation. He launches upright and spins, charging toward the door. Luke steps in front of him just before he reaches it, shoving at his chest.

"Stop and think before you charge out there."

"That fucker is going to die, Luke. You don't know what he did. Move."

"Dimitri, stop and think," Luke orders. "We need that information and he's the only person who can provide it. If you kill him, it's all going to go with him. Think about it."

Dimitri stops and steps back, glaring at Luke for a second. With a sigh, he reaches up, running his hand through his hair. "I can't stand in front of that piece of shit and let him speak without wanting to cut his fuckin' balls off."

"You have to, just until we have our information. Then I won't hold you back."

Dimitri nods.

My entire world stops spinning. He's going to take his side for long enough to get information. My ears begin to ring as I push to my feet. How. Dare. He? The one moment in my life I needed someone to back me, and he's going to actually interact with that man just for information.

Information about Hendrix, no doubt.

Once again, revenge comes first. I walk toward the door, my hands trembling. I get to it before Dimitri realizes I've moved. "Whoa, Jess, where are you goin'?"

I turn to him just as soon as I've opened the door. "Where am I going?" I begin in a whisper that quickly turns to a scream. "Where am I going? I'm going to fucking leave, that's where I'm going. How dare you take his side? How dare you support the monster that he is? I thought . . . I thought you understood better than anyone but I was wrong. You're no better than him. Revenge is all you care about."

"Luke, get hold of her," Dimitri murmurs to Luke, his eyes still on mine. He knows I'm about to run.

He's right.

I turn and I bolt out into the crowd. I hear him bellow something, and I hear Luke's answering yell. I honestly don't think I'll be able to get out of the fighting ring before Luke gets hold of me, but I have an advantage—I'm tiny and Luke is huge. I shove through the people, squeezing through gaps. The minute I reach the door, I leap out into the cool night air.

Like the heavens have opened for me, I notice a cab parked on the side of the road. I charge toward it and swing open the door. Someone who was waiting in line spits a curse at me, but it doesn't halt me. I need to get out of here. The moment I have the door shut, I turn to the driver, "Can you get me out of here, please?"

The cab driver nods and pulls away. I turn and peer out of the back window just in time to see Luke and Dimitri run out of the club. I duck in my seat, panting. I swallow over and over, trying to keep the bile in my stomach from rising. I didn't really think about my plan, I just knew I had to get out of there. I don't have any money, which means I can't even pay this driver.

I feel panic rise in my chest.

What am I supposed to do? Without money, I've got no hope. I remember the phone Dimitri gave me, and with a sudden rush of desperation, I yank it out. I know Hendrix's number back to front, but the chances of him answering it are so slim it's almost not worth trying. But I have to try—he's possibly the only chance I've got right now, slim or not. I begin to dial his number when a text message flashes on the screen.

Dimitri—*I will find you, Jess. Come back to the club. We need to talk.*

I shake my head, holding back my tears as I finish dialing Hendrix. Taking a deep breath, I press the phone to my ear. It begins to ring. That's a good sign. If he was out of service, it wouldn't ring at all. I begin losing hope, though, when it rings and rings, with no answer. I'm just about to hang up when I hear the distinct clicking sound of someone answering.

"Yeah?"

Relief floods my body and I lose hold of the tears I was keeping back.

"H-H-H-Hendrix?"

"Jess?" he rasps. "Fuck, Jess, is that you?"

"It's me," I whisper, trembling.

"Are you okay? Where are you? Tell me where you are?"

"I'm . . . I'm . . ."

I have no idea where I am. I lean forward and say to the cab driver, "What city are we in?"

He gives me a look over his shoulder and mutters, "Los Angeles."

Really?

"Did you hear that?" I whisper.

"I'm docked there too," he says, his voice a sound I've missed so much. "We've been tracking Dimitri. I didn't think he'd be stupid enough to bring you onto land . . ."

"I'm in a cab, I just ran from him. I've got no money, Hendrix."

"Tell him to bring you to Hotel Bel-Air. I'll meet you there."

"Is Indi with you?" I whisper.

"No, kid, she's on the ship still. Be there in twenty."

I hang up the phone and tell the cab driver where to take me. It takes us a solid forty minutes to reach the hotel, but the moment we arrive I can see Hendrix standing out front, pacing. My heart swells and more tears stumble down my cheeks. Hendrix turns to the cab, and his eyes widen. I open the door and get out, and I see his chest exhale. He was holding his breath.

I rush over to him and he takes big strides to get to me. The minute I'm in front of him, he leans down and lifts me up, scooping me into the biggest hug he's ever given me. "Fuck, Jess, I'm so sorry." He holds me tight, so tightly I can hardly breathe, but I don't care. Seeing him again is all I wanted. My tears soak his shirt and I take a minute to inhale, remembering him the way I know him.

"Excuse me?" the cab driver says. "That's eighty dollars."

Hendrix lets me go and shoves a hand into his pocket, pulling out two fifty dollar bills. "Keep the change."

"Why . . . thanks," the cab driver says, getting back into the car and driving off.

Hendrix turns back to me, and his hands reach out and take mine. Then he starts turning my arms over and staring at them. He's seeing if I'm hurt.

"I'm okay, he didn't hurt me," I whisper.

"Come inside, we have to talk."

I nod and follow him inside. He tells the girl at the front desk that he wants a room for me, and when we have the keys we head up. On the elevator, he turns to me and cups my cheeks. "Fuckin' scared, every fuckin' second."

"I know," I whisper. "I'm okay."

The elevator dings and we both exit, heading to the room. When we get in, I take only a moment to look around. It's a nice room, with a king-sized bed and warm tones. The bathroom is a warm caramel-type color and there's a massive bath. There's a small fridge and a kettle, as well as a two-person sofa. A set of large sliding doors open onto a deck with a great view.

"Sit," Hendrix orders.

I walk over to the sofa and I sit. He drops down beside me and turns to face me. His beautiful eyes scan my face. "What happened?"

I swallow. "He took me on the ship for a few weeks, looking for you. He couldn't find you so we came back here. He fights and . . . that's where we were tonight. It was going fine until . . ."

"Until what, Jess?"

I feel more tears slide down my cheeks. Hendrix reaches over and takes my hand. "Until what?"

"He's still alive, Hendrix. I saw him."

He shakes his head. "Who?"

"My foster father."

He sucks in a breath. "Fuck, Jess. Did he hurt you?"

"No, he was giving Dimitri information. I took the chance to run."

I don't tell him all of what went on tonight because it's just details he doesn't need to know. I don't want him to be upset with me. I don't want him to think that I've betrayed him for kissing Dimitri. Well, for even feeling anything but hatred for Dimitri.

"Can he find you?"

"Which one?" I laugh, but it's broken and sad.

"Both."

"No, I don't think so."

"Then you need to come back with me. We'll figure out a way to bring Dimitri down and—"

My phone rings suddenly, cutting him off. I feel my eyes widen and I pull it from my pocket. It's Dimitri. I stare at the screen and then hit reject. Before I can hide it, a message flashes on the screen.

Dimitri—*Baby, hide as much as you want. I'll track you.*

"Baby?" Hendrix breathes.

Oh. Shit.

I drop the phone and dare to look up at him. His expression is wild.

"It's not—"

"Not what!" he roars. "I've been fuckin' lookin' for you and you've been shackin' up with my psycho son?"

"It's not like that, Hendrix. I've wanted you to find me more than anything."

"Are you sure about that?"

My eyes water and my lips tremble. Hendrix sighs and drops his head into his hands.

"You need to be honest with me, Jess. I can't help you if you're not honest," he manages, even though his voice is strained and full of disappointment.

I open my mouth and croak out, "I'm being honest, Hendrix. I've wanted you to find me. Hell, I tried to kill him so you wouldn't risk your own life. For you to think I'd just forget you . . ."

"I'm sorry," he says, turning to me. "I didn't mean to yell at you. But shit, I've been beside myself . . . thinking he was hurtin' you."

"He didn't," I whisper.

"I have to end this with him, Jess."

I nod. "I'm aware of that, but if you do it now, he'll kill you. Or, worse, you'll kill him."

"He's upending my life, he took something that was mine. I can't just let this go on."

I shake my head, reaching over and taking his hand. "Then let me stay."

"What?" he says, eyes wide. "Over my dead fuckin' body."

"Listen to me, Hendrix," I plead. "He . . . we've grown close. I'm beginning to understand him, to break down his barriers. I think . . . well . . . I hope that I can change his mind about all this. If I can spend more time with him, then I can maybe get him to come to you in a calmer frame of mind."

"It's too big a risk," he says, shaking his head.

"No, it's not. He won't hurt me, Hendrix."

"You don't know his level of fucked up, Jess. I can't trust that he won't snap."

I laugh bitterly. "But I do understand his level of fucked up, because I'm the same."

Hendrix's eyes soften. "Shit, Jess. This is dangerous."

"It's not. He won't hurt me."

"Do you care about him? Is that why you want to stay?"

I look away, staring out the window. "I do care about him, yes. But more than that, I care about you, Hendrix. I don't want either of you hurt. He's damaged, he thinks you left him to get hurt. You're angry because he's interfered in your life and started a war. If I go back with you, it will fuel his rage. If I go back to him, I might just have a chance to calm this."

He grumbles and runs his fingers down his chin. "Shit, Jess, you're asking me to put a lot of trust in you here."

"I need you to do this for me, Hendrix. Please?"

He meets my gaze. "If he hurts you . . ."

"He won't."

He sighs. "Fine. I'll give you a month. If I don't hear from you by then, I'm coming back for you, Jess. I can't just leave you there . . ."

"I'll do everything I can."

He shakes his head and leans back, then he murmurs, "Don't fall in love with him."

I stare at him. "Pardon?"

"I can see it, in your eyes. There's a connection forming but it's not a healthy one. He took you . . . for revenge—"

"I know, Hendrix," I all but snap.

He puts his hands up. "I just want you to see this how it is. I don't want you to go into this blind."

"I'm not blind, Hendrix."

"Then answer me this: If I was in front of him, and you were too, and something bad was happening to you but he had the chance to take me out, do you believe he would sacrifice that to save you?"

My eyes water again, because I can't honestly answer that. I don't know what Dimitri would do.

"I can't answer that, Hendrix, because I don't honestly know. But I believe there's a chance. I need you to let me have this."

"And I'm giving it to you. Just don't close your eyes, Jessie. Keep them wide open."

I smile at his pet name for me—it's been a while since he's used it. At my smile, he smiles too and pulls me in for a hug.

"We've been worried about you. Indi has missed you."

"I've missed her too. Tell her I'm okay. Tell her I said hi."

"After she beats me, you mean?"

I giggle softly. "Yeah."

We sit quietly for a moment, before I decide to ask him a question I've been needing an answer to.

"Hendrix?"

"Hmmm?"

"You weren't out on the ocean. He looked for you, for two weeks . . . but you weren't there."

"I didn't doubt Dimitri's sources, Jessie. I knew he would be able to find me if he needed to, so leaving myself open was stupid. I needed to be smart and hit him on land—where he least expected it. I knew if he went out there and couldn't find me, he would go back. So, I was tracking him. I kept myself hidden, but I have my contacts too. When he was heading toward Los Angeles, I knew he'd stop so I came too. I was tracking his location when you called."

"I thought as much," I admit. "I didn't think you would have just left yourself open. Well . . . that's not entirely true. There was a time there, when I saw all Dimitri's weapons and contacts, I worried for you."

He chuckles. "Don't worry about me. I'm the ultimate, baby."

I laugh. "I'm happy you're here and I got to let you know I'm okay."

"Me too, Jessie. Me too."

~

Hendrix leaves after we eat something together. I hold back the tears as he walks out the door, promising to keep tracking me. He's placed a device on my phone that will allow him to follow me if he needs to get to me at any time. He's given me a month to change his mind, otherwise he's coming back in to take me out. No doubt Dimitri too.

I sit on the bed and lean against the soft pillows. My mind won't sway from Dimitri, and my heart won't stop aching. He hurt me. He doesn't realize how much. I know I have to call him, though, because he will turn this city upside down trying to find me if I don't. I pull out the phone and stare down at the thirty missed calls on the screen.

With a deep breath, I lift the phone and dial his number, pressing it to my ear.

"Where the fuck are you?" he barks the minute he answers.

"If you're going to talk to me like that, I'm not telling you."

He's silent and takes a deep breath. "Jess, where are you?"

I give him the address for the hotel.

"How did you get into a hotel?"

I hesitate. Shit, I never even thought of that.

"I, um, knew my credit card details by heart. They accepted it."

"Yeah," he says hesitantly. "Well, I'll be there in a bit."

"Okay."

I hang up the phone and place it beside me, then I lean back into the pillows. I honestly don't know what I'll feel when I see Dimitri. My chest is constricting, my heart is pounding, and my head is telling me Hendrix is right. I close my eyes and focus on taking a few deep breaths. It's important I don't break down, that I approach Dimitri right about all this.

Or I'll fail—and failing isn't an option.

"Jess!"

I jerk my eyes open, and it seems like half an hour has passed in a blur. I must have drifted off. I stumble out of the bed and hurry to the door, swinging it open. Dimitri is standing, wearing a pair of faded jeans, a tight black tee, and unlaced boots. It looks like he's just thrown some clothes on and run out. I stare up at his face, and gasp. His eye is black and his jaw is bruising.

"You're hurt."

He shrugs. "It happens. Can I come in?"

I nod, pushing the door open. He steps in, glancing around the room before turning to me.

"We need to talk."

"Yeah," I whisper. "I know."

I sit on the edge of the bed and he stands in front of me, shoving his hands into his pockets.

"I fucked up, Jess."

127

I look up at him with wide eyes. "What?"

"I said I fucked up. I should have killed that son of a bitch without hesitation."

I look away, feeling my cheeks heat. "Your revenge came first, Dimi."

"Yeah, but I said I fucked up."

I look up at him, and he stares right into my eyes. I can see the regret there. I sigh and rub my hands over my legs.

I hesitate for a moment, but I know this might be the only chance I have of getting things out of Dimitri that I haven't been able to before. "Can I ask you something?"

He takes a step forward and sits beside me. "Yeah."

"Will you answer me honestly?"

He sits on my question for a minute, before answering, "Yeah."

I gather my courage and then I speak. "If I was in front of you, and I was in trouble, and Hendrix appeared too, what would you do?"

"I don't follow," he says, looking puzzled.

"Would you take the chance to get Hendrix or would you save me?"

He narrows his eyes, like he's shocked. A look of pure horror crosses his face.

"What kind of man do you think I am, Jess?" he almost whispers, his voice is so low.

"I . . ."

"Clearly not what I thought," he mutters, standing.

"Dimi," I say, standing too.

He spins around. He's angry now. "The fact that you honestly thought I'd take him over saving you tells me you have learned nothing about me."

"You haven't exactly given me anything other than 'revenge, revenge, revenge'."

He shakes his head, glaring at me. "I won't deny revenge is all I've thought about. But if you were ever in trouble, nothing . . . *nothing* would stop me from fuckin' getting to you."

I feel my body tingle all over.

"It wouldn't?"

He turns and walks to the door. "No, and you shoulda known that."

I rush toward him. "Dimitri, don't just walk out."

He doesn't listen to me.

"You hurt me tonight," I yell, causing him to stop. "You let that . . . that . . . *man* . . . go. You took his side for information. Did you really think I wouldn't question what this is that's between us?"

He spins around. "I'd have never let him touch you."

"It's beside the point!" I yell.

"Fuck, Jess, what do you want from me? I stole you. At what point did I go from being the enemy to fucking Prince Charming?"

I shake my head, letting tears leak out. They run down my cheeks and drip off my chin, but I don't stop them.

"I never said I wanted Prince Charming. Hell, I never even said I wanted the bad guy. I just want honesty, Dimi. I want to know why I'm still here talking to you, when I had the chance to run."

He walks toward me until he stops in front of me. He looks down at me, his blue eyes intense. "You tell me," he breathes. "Why didn't you run?"

I shake my head, staring at him through blurred vision. "Because I can see beyond what everyone else sees. I can see the side to you that you've pushed down. I can see a part of me in *you*. I feel a connection when I'm with you, an understanding . . . but more than anything, I feel you, Dimitri. With everything I am."

Before another word can leave my lips, he lunges forward, wrapping his hands around my shoulders and crushing my body against his. Then his lips descend toward mine. The moment they connect, I forget everything. My knees become weak and I find myself curling my fingers into his shirt, being careful not to touch his chest. He groans and takes a step forward, causing me to take a step backwards.

We hit the bed and tumble down, and the weakness in my body quickly turns to fear as his body slams over mine. To most, this is a beautiful moment. To me, it's pure terror. I gasp and wrench my mouth from his, putting my hands to his chest and shoving him hard. He flinches at my contact, and his body, too, stiffens. He jackknifes off me and stumbles backwards. I sit up, panting.

We both look like we've just relived something awful.

God. How fucked up are we?

I rub my hands over my chest and stare at Dimi, who is looking down at the floor, his fists clenched. It bothered him too, when I touched him. It brought back something he doesn't want to face. Just like his body over mine did. I sigh deeply and drop my head into my hands. What can I say right now to make this better? Is there even a way to make it better?

"Well, aren't we just a picture of fucked up-ness," I mutter.

I lift my head to see Dimitri staring at me, his lip quirking.

"Fucked up-ness?"

"Yeah," I say, lying back on the bed. "Fucked up-ness."

He walks over and surprises me by dropping down onto the bed beside me. We both lie, side by side, staring at the ceiling.

"We make an interesting . . ." I halt, trying to think of a word.

"Couple?" he offers.

"We're not a couple, we can't even fuck."

He makes a choking sound and I glance over to see him grinning. "I can't stand being touched and you can't stand being fucked."

I laugh softly. "Could make for an interesting union."

"Do you want me to fuck you, Jess?"

My cheeks flush. It takes me a moment to answer, because it's not something I ever thought I'd feel. The very idea of sex terrifies me, yet a huge part of my body wants him, so much so that I want to know what it feels like to have a man who's genuine take my body. I know it's different, I know he's not . . . he's not Roger. So, I answer him with full honesty. "Oh, Dimi, yes."

He turns to me, his eyes blazing. "Don't know how we could work it."

I shake my head, struggling to control my breathing. "No, I don't either."

"Most of the women I fuck just lie there, or they ride me with their hands on their legs."

"Thanks for that information," I murmur.

"We can't do those things because you don't want my body over yours . . ."

"It's not that I don't . . . it was just . . . it was how you came over me so fast and—"

"I get it," he interrupts. "I do."

We're both silent. When I turn and look at him, he's watching me, his face gentle but equally lusty. "You can do one thing for me."

"I can?" I whisper. "And what's that?"

"You can kiss me again, baby."

Oh. Yes. That I can do.

I roll toward him and I lean forward, pressing our lips together. He shifts closer to me so we're not touching, but we're close enough that we can kiss comfortably. He starts out with a slow, deep kiss involving some tongue action that has my body burning for him. As things heat up, the kiss turns more intense. My body becomes aware of his, and I find myself wanting to press myself against him. Things ache in my body that only Dimitri could get to ache.

Pulling his mouth from mine, he murmurs, "How about we try something?"

"Oh?" I stammer.

"One thing at a time. One hand."

I stare at him, confused.

"I'll put one hand on you, and you," he takes a deep breath, "can put one on me."

He's going to let me touch him. The very idea of this excites me to no end. I find myself nodding without thinking it through. I don't need to think it through. Feeling Dimitri is something I've thought so much about. I stretch my hand out to him and I can see his skin almost ripple as it gets closer—this is because he's flinching a great deal. I gently lay my fingertips on his side and I just leave them there.

He reaches across, placing his fingers in the exact same area of my body that mine are on his. He's giving me charge. I slowly lean in again, pressing my lips to his. He lets me, opening his mouth to my needy tongue. When our kiss is heated again, I run my fingers down his side just slightly. I can feel his kiss falter, but he doesn't stop me. He just follows the same path with his fingers. My skin breaks out as they lightly graze my body.

I reach the hem of his shirt and I hesitate. I want to take this further, I want to feel him, but I'm terrified. So scared that the moment we take it that step too far, I'll break. I close my eyes, pulling my lips from his and resting my forehead against his. He's panting, I can feel puffs of it blowing out against my cheek.

"Are you okay?" I whisper.

"Yeah."

I don't know if that's a go-ahead or not, but I give it a test. I grip the hem of his shirt and I slowly lift it. I move my head back just a touch and watch his eyes as I lift the shirt up to his chest. He's got them closed and his jaw is tight. He moves, though, allowing me to raise it by lifting his arms. He helps me with the last part of it, and he flicks it onto the floor. Then he takes the hem of mine. I swallow and let him raise it over my head.

I can see my own chest rising and falling as his eyes lower to my breasts. They're covered by a lacey bra that actually does good things for my cleavage. My skin looks so pale next to his beautifully bronzed skin. I lift my eyes to his and see he's now watching me, his expression completely unreadable. I place my trembling fingers back on his side, feeling his warmth radiating through them. He sucks in a breath and stares at me with a pained expression.

"No one has touched my bare skin since . . ."

"Since what?" I whisper.

I know Dimitri was beaten when Hendrix left him at a young age, but I have never been told what else happened. I'm sure, though, without a doubt, that he was assaulted in some way. I just don't know how. There's a reason he's this level of fucked up—I knew it from the moment I met him because I could see behaviors in him that I had in myself after it all happened.

"Nothing. It's just been a long time."

"Dimi . . ."

"Jess, don't."

I won't argue with him. If he doesn't want to tell me, then he doesn't have to. I know better than anyone that pushing something like that never ends well.

"Are you okay with my hand on you?" I whisper.

He nods, reaching across and stroking my side. "And you?"

"Yes, Dimi."

He gives me a half-smile. "I love the sound of your voice when you call me Dimi."

"How so?"

"It changes. You say it with a gentle tone."

I smile and flatten my palm onto his side. He flinches but he doesn't stop me.

"What now?" I ask, swallowing.

"I wanna touch you, Jess. I want my mouth on you in places that have been on my mind for weeks. I want my body inside yours. I want it all, but I want it all with you wanting it as much."

"I want it," I admit. "I'm just . . . I'm scared."

He nods and I can see he understands. "How about we just keep goin' like this, yeah?"

"Yeah."

"Goin' to touch you more now, baby, because my hands don't wanna stay still and it's takin' everything I am to hold them back."

I nod, moving my hand down and over his chest. His body is still tense beneath my touch but he allows it. I can feel the muscles under his skin. They're hard, powerful, and completely arousing. Just looking at them has me wanting to roll over and climb on top of him, just so I can see them move. My thoughts are ripped from me when his fingers slide up and over my bra. I shiver.

His fingers graze me ever so slightly, before he gently cups one of my breasts into his hand. I whimper and swallow, staring into his eyes, which haven't left mine. He moves closer, sliding his hand around behind me and finding the clasp. My heart begins to pound and I begin panting. I've never . . . never been exposed willingly to a man. I'm terrified.

"Dimi," I whisper and his fingers pause immediately. "I'm afraid."

"If you want me to stop, I'll stop."

"No," I say, my voice trembling. "I . . ."

"Your voice is trembling, sweetheart."

Sweetheart.

I take a deep breath and say, "It's okay. Please, don't stop."

He gently unclips my bra and it slips off quickly. He unhooks it from my arms and then tosses it onto the ground. Then he stares down at me. His eyes are on my breasts for a solid three minutes before he reaches out and gently strokes his thumb over my nipple. I jerk and he stops immediately.

"Don't stop," I rasp.

It feels so . . . nice. I never imagined how it would feel to have someone touch my breasts. Roger, thankfully, only ever took what he wanted—which was sex—before leaving. He never touched the other parts of my body, so I guess this is one of the parts that isn't tainted by his evil.

He gently takes my nipple between his thumb and forefinger and he rolls it. I gasp as little bolts of pleasure shoot down my spine, through my belly and into my sex. Oh. My. I see little bumps breaking out over my skin as pleasure takes over. I close my eyes. My hand is still resting against his chest. He rolls my nipple again and I find myself curving toward him.

Then I feel him shift. I don't open my eyes until I feel a warm mouth close over my nipple. Then they pop open and I stare down at the thick mass of dark hair. I gently reach out and tangle my fingers in it, then I drop my head back and moan as he flicks the top of my nipple with his tongue, circling it, occasionally nipping it and doing other wonderful things until my sex is clenching so hard it's almost painful.

"Dimi," I gasp. "E-e-e-enough."

He pulls his mouth from my nipple and looks up at me. His lips are wet and so beautifully red. Oh. I want them. I reach down, running my thumb over his bottom lip. "It's my turn."

His brows raise. "You're going to lick my nipples?"

I burst out laughing.

"No," I giggle hysterically. "I meant to touch you."

He chuckles and lies down. I notice the peak in his pants and my eyes widen. Whoa. I knew he was not lacking down below but . . . wow. His pants are really straining.

"Did you want a picture?"

I jerk my eyes up and smile sheepishly. "Oh . . . I . . ."

"Baby," he murmurs with a grin. "If you want to stare at my cock, then you can stare at my cock."

Oh.

Wow.

Hearing him use the word cock has all that clenching starting back up again. I lean forward, sick of waiting, ready to take the plunge. I press my lips to his neck and he stiffens. "Baby, not there."

I move them quickly, moving them up his jaw instead. This seems to please him, because he lets out a deep groan. When I reach his lips, I crush mine against his. His hand moves to my hip, curling his fingers around it and tugging me toward him. He deepens the kiss, while his fingers move over my shorts. He reaches for the button in front and flips it open quickly.

"Get them off," he orders.

I nod and shift out of my shorts until it's just me in my panties. "You too," I breathe.

"I've got nothing on underneath."

"I don't care," I murmur. "Off."

He jerks his pants down and off, and I hear my own loud gasp. Wow, holy shit, wow. Dimitri naked is . . . shit . . . wow. There are no other words. He's a mass of corded muscle, bronze skin, and lickable abs. I let my eyes travel down to his cock, and my heart begins to pound. I was right, he's not lacking down below. His fingers curl around my hip and bring me back closer to him.

His mouth finds mine again as his fingers begin to travel over my body, down my breasts, over my hips, around my thighs, and back up again. I'm aching for him after a matter of minutes and I push my body closer, giving him an indication that I want more. I need more. He slides his lips away from my mouth and lets them travel down my jaw and neck. He reaches my collarbone and sucks gently on it.

"I want you to . . . touch me, Dimi. Please."

He makes me a rumbling sound against my chest as he moves down.

"On it, baby."

He slides farther, pressing his mouth against my breasts again, warming them right back up before moving lower down. He presses kisses to my belly as he continues down to my pubic bone. I can feel his warm breath against my sex and I bite my lower lip, feeling a mix of emotions. Fear, arousal, uncertainty . . .

"Say stop, I'll stop. Do you hear me?"

I nod, even though he can't see it.

"Baby?"

"Y-y-yes."

"Spread your legs, darlin'."

My legs are trembling as I let them fall open. Oh God, oh . . .

"Wider."

I let them just fall to the sides, holding nothing back. Dimitri growls his appreciation and lowers his mouth to my exposed sex. The moment his warm lips touch my pussy, I gasp. It's something I'd never imagined in my wildest fantasies. He curls his arms around my legs and uses that leverage to pull my pussy closer to his mouth. His tongue slides between my folds and flicks my clit.

My back arches as a sudden bolt of pleasure radiates through my body.

"D-D-Dimi," I gasp. "Oh God."

He sucks my clit into his mouth deeply, before continuing to flick it with his tongue. His breath is warm against my flesh and his arms are tight around my thighs. The whole experience is exhilarating. I never want it to end. He lifts his hand and brings his fingers up, sliding them around my entrance. My body stiffens the moment he slips one in.

"Dimi," I cry out. "I . . . I don't . . ."

He removes his finger and lifts his head, looking directly at me. "Won't hurt you baby, but if you don't want it, then we aren't gonna do it."

I stare at him, my chest rising and falling, my body wound up to the absolute max. I trust him, I know he won't hurt me. I also know I don't want to spend the rest of my life being afraid. He's not Roger. He is not Roger.

"I want you to," I whisper.

His eyes scan my face, but he nods and moves back down, closing his mouth over my clit once more. His fingers dance around my entrance, stroking and sliding, before he slowly presses one inside. My back arches again and I grit my teeth. It's Dimitri. Dimitri. He curls his finger and I feel him stroke over that soft bundle of nerves that has my body coming alive.

It's Dimitri. Yes. It's Dimitri.

He slides his finger in and out while his mouth continues to consume me. I get to the point where my body is trembling and my eyes are rolling backwards as I feel an explosion hanging on the edge. With one final flick of Dimitri's tongue and a thrust of his finger, I'm coming. Oh. I'm coming. I cry out his name and my body jerks with each beautiful burst of release that travels through my body.

Before I know what's happening, Dimitri has slid his body back up mine and is settled between my legs. I can feel his cock poking against me, ready, wanting. I feel my body tighten and I shake my head from side to side. "Dimi . . ."

"It's okay," he murmurs against my neck as he nuzzles in. "Slowly, remember?"

I swallow and clutch the sheets beside me. His cock is pressing tightly against me, causing just a touch of pressure within my core. He strokes a finger down my cheek. "I love the pink in your cheeks right now."

"I didn't know you could do such good things with your tongue."

He smiles, showing me that adorable dimple. "You just wait until I show you what I can do with the rest of my body."

I shake my head, grinning. "Cocky much?"

He rotates his hips letting me know he's right there, ready. "Oh yeah."

"Hmmmm," I murmur, reaching up and splaying my fingers against his chest. "What does the tattoo mean?"

He stares down at the tattoo, causing his thick hair to tickle my face. I giggle. He looks back up at me with a lazy half-grin. "Something funny?"

"Your hair," I say, reaching up and tugging it softly.

"Yeah, no idea why I keep it long."

"I like it."

He tucks a hand under my hip and snuggles us closer. "Mmmmm."

"The tattoo?" I whisper.

"It's just a symbol of my struggles."

I nod, figuring he doesn't want to say much more, so I don't push.

The phone by the bedside rings, making us both turn our heads and look at it quizzically. "Who would be ringing you now?" he asks.

I shrug. "I don't know."

My heart flutters. I hope it's not Hendrix. I shift from underneath Dimi and with a sigh, he rolls off. I reach over for the phone and answer it. "Um, hello?"

"Dimi with you, Jess?"

It's Luke.

"Oh, Luke, hey. Yeah, he is."

"Throw him on?"

I hand the phone to Dimitri, who takes it and presses it against his ear. He's got a sheet up to his hips, but it's pitching one hell of a tent. I smile and flush.

"Yeah?" Dimitri says down the phone.

He listens for a second and then sighs.

"Right, I'll be there in an hour."

He hangs the phone up and rolls to me. "I got another fight."

"But . . . you just had one," I say, pointing to his bruising eye.

He shrugs. "It'll be fine. I gotta go."

I nod, but I can't help my frown.

He raises a brow. "You goin' to come with me?"

I look up at him as he gets out of the bed and leans down, pulling his pants back on.

"I-is he going to be there?"

He gives me a gentle look. "I don't know."

"Do you trust me here?"

"Should I trust you here?" he throws back, but he's not being nasty about it.

"I'm not going to leave you, Dimi," I say softly.

He stares at me for a long moment. "I'll send Luke over. He can wait in the lobby."

"You don't trust me," I sigh.

He doesn't answer me, how can he? The fact is, he doesn't trust me. Why would he? In his eyes, I'm still here against my will.

"Just want you protected," he murmurs. "I'll be back in a few hours. We'll spend the night and then head back to my house in the morning."

"We're going back to your house?"

He nods. "Got more fights."

I sigh but I don't bother arguing. "Okay."

He cups my chin and tilts my head up, pressing a kiss to my forehead.

"I won't be long."

He pulls out a cellphone as he's jerking his shirt on, and I hear him ordering Luke to head over. Then he turns to me.

"He's coming over now—he'll get here the same time that I get there. You'll only be alone an hour."

"It's fine. You didn't need to bring him over at all."

He tugs on his boots and nods to my phone sitting on the bedside table. "You need me, use it."

I nod.

He looks hard at me, and I know the expression on my face is that of disappointment. For more reasons than one. The first is that he's leaving. The second is that he's still fighting for information.

"A few hours."

I don't bother nodding. I just get out of the bed and head into the bathroom.

"Later, Dimi."

I hear him sigh and leave the room.

That didn't go how I planned.

Not at all.

CHAPTER NINETEEN

Dimitri

Boss, you should know we got some information on Jess tonight."

I turn to Peter, my second in charge for the night. He's not much older than me, but he's a damned loyal worker.

"Hit me with it." I say, walking to my locker and opening it.

"After she ran, you know, obviously, you sent someone after her. He had problems communicating back. That's why we're only getting the information now. He said he had troubles with his phone."

I don't entirely know if that's true. Ted, the man I sent after the cab she jumped in, isn't the most reliable of sources. The fucker probably didn't even take his phone.

"Anyway, he contacted us just after you left to return here. He gave us a big bullshit story as to why it took so long, but that's not important. He said he got to the hotel just after Jess, because his driver had to do a lap of the block to get a parking spot. She was already inside by the time he managed to find somewhere to park. He said he waited, unable to call it in because of his phone. He said about an hour after he sat, someone came out of the hotel."

"Someone?" I ask, strapping my knuckles.

"Boss," he hesitates. "He said he saw Hendrix come out."

My entire body jerks. Hendrix? Fucking Hendrix?

"What the motherfuck was that cunt doing there?"

He shakes his head. "I don't know, he just said it was most definitely him."

He was in her room with her. She saw him. Everything in my body turns to ice. I just gave her a part of myself and she was with Hendrix. God, I'm such a fucking idiot. She's probably plotting with him. It's why she's not leaving, why she's not running. It's how she got the fucking hotel room.

Anger boils over and I drive my fist into the locker so hard a massive dint appears straightaway. Blood trickles out of a split in my knuckles and the throbbing pain doesn't ease the one forming in my heart.

"Get. Her. Here. Now."

"Yes, sir."

So help me fuckin' God, this isn't going to end well.

She betrayed me. Fucking betrayed me.

She will pay.

∽

Jess

"Jess!"

Luke is pounding on my door. I sigh, wondering why the hell he's suddenly so desperate to get to me. I've just finished a shower and was looking forward to lying in bed and getting some sleep. With a growl, I walk over and swing it open. He's staring at me, his eyes hard. There's something behind them—I can't pinpoint what it is but it's not a happy look.

I've gotten to know Luke a little better since I've been here, and there are times, although occasional, when he actually smiles at me. Now, he looks as though he wants to rip my head off. I really don't understand why. Was I supposed to let him in? Is he angry about having to stand outside until Dimi gets back? I put my hand up on the doorframe and stare right back at him.

"What's wrong?"

"Time to go. Now."

I shake my head, sure I've heard him wrong. "What?"

"You heard me," he barks. "It's time to go. Let's move."

He reaches out and takes my hand, tugging me. "Wait!" I cry. "Let me get changed."

He lets me go and growls, "Hurry up."

I turn and quickly change back into my clothes and then I throw my hair up into a ponytail before rushing back to the door.

"Why the hurry?" I ask as Luke takes my arm again, pulling me out.

"I'll let the boss speak to you."

I shake my head and let him pull me down to a waiting car. He opens the door and I get into the back quickly, pulling on my seatbelt. Luke walks around after slamming my door loudly, and jumps into the passenger seat. A man I don't know is driving. I cross my arms and stare out of the window, not quite sure what to make of the sudden outburst. I decide, until I can speak to Dimitri, there's no point in saying anything. So, I sit back and stay silent until we pull up at Dimitri's house.

I'm surprised we've come here, and even more so that Dimitri didn't come and get me, or even call. When the car comes to a stop, I climb out and walk up to the front door. Luke catches up in a mere second, and I can feel his presence behind me. God, why is he so close? Is there any need for that? I pick up my pace and head into the main living area.

Dimitri is standing by the window. His fists are down by his side and he seems to be panting. Is he angry at me? Luke clears his throat and I watch as Dimi turns and pins me with his scathing glare. He's angry, I was right . . . I just don't know what he's angry about. Luke turns and walks out of the room, leaving me alone with him. I warily take a step forward, unsure what the hell is going on.

"Who got your room for you tonight?" Dimitri growls, his voice low and throaty.

I shake my head. "I did, I told you that."

Suddenly his fist flies out and smashes into a nearby lamp. It soars off the table and smashes onto the floor. I flinch and take a step back.

"Don't you fucking lie to me!" he roars, storming toward me. "I know, Jessica. I *know*."

I swallow and try hard to steady my breathing. "I don't know what—"

"Enough!" he bellows. "I know Hendrix was with you tonight. Did you think I was fucking stupid?"

He's panting. His jaw is tight. His body is rigid. He's wild. No, he's gone beyond wild. He's lost it, completely. I wrap my arms around myself, struggling for a decent answer. I don't know what I can say to him. He'll never believe that I basically begged Hendrix not to hurt him.

"I saw him," I whisper. "Yes."

"You fucking lied to me!" he bellows. "Not only that, you betrayed me. I trusted you."

"No you didn't," I suddenly cry, feeling my skin prickle all over. "You never fucking trusted me, Dimi. Not for a second."

"Did I give you a phone?"

"A phone you were going to take off me the moment you finished your fight. The only reason I got in that cab is because I was running from you, because you betrayed me."

His face turns stony. "You let him in and you played me like a fucking fool."

"The only person playing you like a fool, Dimitri," I tell him, "is you. You're living so much in the past that you can't pull your head out of your ass and see the future."

He stiffens and his back goes ramrod straight. "My business is just that, mine! It was never yours."

"Then why the hell did you take me? You made it my business the day you took me from my family and used me as a pawn in your sick games. When did you ever think I would change my mind about Hendrix? Did you truly believe I would bring him to you? Or that I'd stop fighting to make sure you didn't hurt him?"

"What I thought," he grinds out, "is that you understood!"

"I do understand," I yell, my voice shaking. "I understand your need to close something, I understand your need to feel okay again. I understand how it feels, but what I don't understand is the need to ruin someone's life, and not just one person, but two. You're taking away from Indi if you hurt him. She's a gentle, beautiful girl and she loves him. You haven't stopped to think, if you take him from her you'll be no better than he is."

He jerks and his breathing deepens. "You. Know. Nothing. About. Me."

"I know more than you think!" I scream, shaking my hands. "I know what happened to you, Dimitri."

"No!" he roars. "What you know is what he told you. Did he tell you what they did to me?"

"They beat you, I know, and I'm sorry but—"

"They fucking raped me!" he bellows, slamming his fist into the wall, splitting it wide open. Blood pours from the wound. "They held me down and one by one they fucking raped me. I was fifteen. There were ten of them. You know fucking nothing about me."

I flinch and gasp. I knew Dimitri had had a hard time, I knew he'd got beaten and I thought there might have been some sort of sexual assault but ten men? I'd had no idea. I open my mouth but nothing comes out. My hands tremble and I press one to my throat, trying to breathe. Dimitri is staring at me, his entire body shaking. He's ready to rip someone apart. That someone is likely to be me.

"I . . . I . . ."

"You've got nothing," he growls, his voice barely above a whisper. "Nothing you can say can make it better. It's his fault it happened and it's his fault I stayed there and had to deal with it."

"You're wrong about that," I say, my voice cracking. "The reason it happened is because of your mom—"

"Don't you ever fucking speak about my mother!"

"I don't mean to insult your mother, Dimitri," I say very carefully and very gently. "But have you ever stopped, even for a second, and thought about why Hendrix ran? He married her at a young age; she was tangled up in some seriously bad shit. He ended up having to take the law out onto the ocean so he could deal with the problems she had created. He had no choice—her life and yours were in danger. Then he found out you had been beaten and . . . h-h-h—"

"Raped," he snarls. "Fucking raped. Say it."

I swallow, unable to answer him. So I continue, "He found out you had been beaten and he found out the problems weren't going to go away. Soon it would have got worse. Soon she

147

would have put you in the position where you would have been killed. He had someone take her out and the bad men around you, too. When he went to the hospital, you'd heard of your mother's death and you didn't know the full story. You hated him. Despised him. That's not to say he shouldn't have stayed and fought, because he should have, but he did everything he did because he loved you."

He's staring at me, just staring. There's no expression on his face. I expect him to abuse me, to tell me I'm a liar and I'm wrong, but he doesn't. Instead he walks straight past me and disappears from the room. I exhale loudly and lower to my knees, wrapping my arms around myself. God, what have I done? I've hurt him. I've ruined every tiny piece of a relationship we'd managed to create.

How am I going to fix this?

~

I wait for half an hour, then another. He doesn't come back. I slowly walk from the room and head to the bedroom he made me stay in when I first got here. The halls are empty, and no one seems to be around. I'm just about to enter my room when I hear the sound of water running. I turn my focus to what I know is Dimitri's room. My heart burns and I find myself turning toward the sound.

He might hate me but I need to know he's okay.

I open the door quietly and peer into the room. I see the light coming from under the door to his bathroom. I hesitate, knowing I should really just turn back. I can't, though. I have to check on him. It's my fault he's in there. It's my fault he's broken. I let him down, there's no excuse for that. I reach the bathroom door and take the handle, swallowing down the anxiety rising in my chest.

I shove the door open softly and step in. I'm faced with a cloud of steam. I feel it stick to my skin as I step in farther. I draw closer to the shower and see Dimitri standing in it. My heart breaks in two. He has his back to me, and he's completely, beautifully naked. His arms are crossed and pressed on the wall in front of him, and his head is hanging between them.

I take the biggest risk I've ever taken in my life to date.

I strip off and I step into the shower. I reach out with trembling fingers and touch his shoulder. He flinches, but not enough. He knew I was there. Slowly he turns, and I feel my knees buckle with pure agony when I see his face. He's got red, glassy eyes and he looks grief-stricken. He's shed a few tears. Not a lot, but a few. For a man like Dimitri, that is a massive thing.

"I'm so sorry," I whisper.

What else is there to say?

His eyes scan my face and I watch as a tear escapes from the corner of his eye. I reach up and catch it before it blends with the water coursing down to drip off his chin, and his eyes follow my fingers. I lift them and cup his cheek. He closes his eyes, almost as though he's in pain, but he allows me to keep my hand there.

"I made a mistake," I whisper. "I'm sorry, Dimi. I didn't know how your life has been, but I should have told you I saw Hendrix. I will tell you where he is, I'll let you do this your way, but I need you to understand something first. I need you to really, really think about what I am saying. To you, Hendrix is a monster. To me, Dimi, he's the only family I have. He saved my life. He gave me a second chance. He didn't have to do that. He didn't have to let me find my sunshine. I know he let you down and for that, I'm truly sorry. But it was never up to him to be the one that made sure you were okay. It was up to your momma, and she failed. You can hate him—I couldn't and wouldn't ask you to change who you are for me. But I can't . . . I can't stand by and watch you hurt the only family I have left. I love him, Dimi. Not in the way I'm learning to love you. No, I love him in the way everyone should love their family. So, if you want to know where he is, I'll tell you. But I can't stand by and watch you take the only thing I have left."

I turn once I'm finished, and I lift a fist and shove a tear from my cheek. I'm just about to step out of the shower when Dimitri's hand lashes out and he jerks me back. I spin around and face him, my vision blurred with my tears. His finger raises up and he swipes them from my cheek. Then he moves his hands to cup my face. He's never touched me so gently, never looked at me with such . . . passion. Slowly, as if the world has stopped turning and it's only the two of us in it, he leans down and presses his lips to mine.

And he kisses me.

He doesn't kiss me like he's kissed me before. He kisses me like I'm the last breath he'll ever take. He kisses me like I'm the only reason he wakes up every day. He kisses me like I *matter*. His hands move from my cheeks and slide down my neck, causing little shivers to break out all over my body. When they reach my shoulders, he uses them to bring me closer, pressing my naked body to his.

I can feel him there, ready for me.

I want him, but not here. Right now, I just want this to be about him. I want him to know that all I care about in this moment is *him*. I reach up and gently take his shoulders, using them to push us back apart. He looks confused as I slowly spin him around to face the wall again. I step up close, pressing my chest to his back. He shivers. I reach around and place my hands on his belly, stroking my fingers up and down.

"It's not about me, Dimi," I say softly. "It's about you. Let me touch you. Know that I would never, ever hurt you."

He doesn't say anything, but he doesn't move either. He lets me move my hands down his abs, running my fingertips over the hard ridges there. When I reach his pelvis, I hesitate. I want to touch him, but once I do, there's no going back. I'm committing myself to someone like him and someone like him isn't easy. He's damaged and moody and completely fucked up.

But he's also beautiful, loving, and kind.

In a sense, if we go to the basics, he's just like me.

And I'm completely okay with that.

So I keep going. I lower my hands until they graze over his cock. The nerves in my stomach are making me sick, but I keep telling myself that this is what I want. It's not forced. It's not a choice made for me. This is something we both want and need. I reach out and curl my fingers around his cock, feeling the thick, hard length jerk in my grip.

My legs wobble.

I close my eyes and press my cheek to his back as I begin to gently stroke up and down. I can feel his rumble of pleasure radiate through my cheek. I break into tiny little shivers and I tighten my grip, feeling him stiffen as I put pressure on his cock and then release it seconds later. Then I take my thumb and I run it over the tip. The skin is soft and smooth. I never would have imagined I could find this . . . beautiful.

"Jess," he rasps.

"Shhh," I soothe, gently picking up my pace.

My hand runs up and down his length, stopping occasionally to give his head attention. His entire body is stiff and he's panting with every stroke I make. He's making little noises and every now and then he murmurs my name. I hear him say "Baby" before I feel his cock swell in my hand. Seconds later, I feel hot spurts of arousal hit my hand and get washed away with water.

His groans continue and his head drops back, tickling my cheeks with his long, thick hair. His hands hit the wall with another garbled grunt and he jerks his cock harder into my hand. My entire body swells with want. I need him. I want to let him in. I want to feel what it's like to have a man like Dimitri surrounding me.

I need it like I need air.

It's finally time.

Time to let myself go.

CHAPTER TWENTY

Dimitri

She's so fucking beautiful. I want her more than I want air. I should hate her, should feel that rage burning in my chest, but the only thing burning is my need to taste her, to be inside her, to have her surrounding me. Especially when she's watching me with those big, green eyes. I know she feels guilty, and a big part of me thinks that's exactly what she should feel, but a bigger part, the part I'm just discovering again, tells me she is the best thing that could ever happen to me.

My mind is spinning with this influx of new emotions. I'm not used to feeling anything but a soul-crushing need for revenge. Hearing her spill the truth ripped me to shreds. I don't know if she's just saying what she thinks I want to hear, but it tugged at something inside me. It cracked my wall, just slightly. Now I don't know what to do. How am I supposed to give up the only thing that seems to keep me stable and calm?

"Come here," I murmur as I back toward the bed.

I don't know what my next move is, but tonight, right here with her, I know exactly what I need. And by the look on her face, she needs it as much. I keep my eyes locked on hers as she takes a nervous step toward me. I extend my hand and she timidly places one of hers in mine. Jess is always so determined and funny, but she looks like she's about to throw up. I know how scary it is for her. I remember the first time I took the leap and gave myself to someone.

"What are you thinking?" she asks, studying my face.

"About the first time I had sex after . . ." I trail off. I hate that word. Fucking hate it.

Jess's eyes soften. "Tell me about it."

She sits on the bed and I drop down beside her.

"Not sure it's going to give you a great deal of confidence, baby," I murmur, making tiny circles on her palm with my fingertip.

"I want to know anyway."

I focus on her hand as I speak. I've never told anyone this story, and I'm certainly not about to share it with anyone else but her. It's not something I'm proud of.

"I was seventeen. I was at the peak of my fucked up-ness."

She smiles at my use of her word, and I can't help but grin back.

"I met this girl at a club one night. She was blond, pretty, ready for a fuck. I was underage but she didn't know. A bunch of us had managed to sneak into the club. I was a good size for my age. I didn't look seventeen. Anyway, that's beside the point. I danced with her, drank with her and somehow found myself back at her hotel room. I was so drunk I didn't think it would matter. I thought I wouldn't remember. We began messing around and I seemed to be taking it well, so we went further. Mid-way through, she was riding me when I realized what was really happening. Memories started flashing in my head and I freaked out. It was like I blacked out and forgot where I was and who I was with. I came about to see that I was shaking her. My hands were on her shoulders and I was shaking the absolute shit out of her. It was fucked up. After that, it took a long time to get into it. I didn't trust anyone and then—"

"Then?" she asks, cutting me off.

"Then I met Macy."

I see the way her face flashes. She's jealous.

"Who's Macy?"

"I was with her for about two years. From nineteen to twenty-one. She was the first person to break through my barrier. She taught me to . . ." I stare at her, noticing her cheeks are pink, so I pick my words carefully, "To . . . be with a woman."

"She was important to you," she says. It's not a question, but a fact.

"I remember the first time she put her hands on me, I flipped out," I say, sighing. "I was so crazy I couldn't stand the idea of having someone's fingers on me. It took her a solid year to be able to run her hand down my face."

"That must have been hard."

I nod. "I'm forever grateful to her, though. She helped me past it. I still can't deal with being touched, but I don't flip out like I used to. God knows she was a strong girl, putting up with me."

"She must have loved you," Jess says, her voice soft and low.

I shake my head. "In her own way, yes, but it wasn't a deep, binding love. She felt for me, she wanted to help me, but I think a big part of her knew she could never be with me. I was too much work, even for her."

"I think she must have cared about you a great deal more than you think, if she tried to help you that much."

I nod. "Yeah."

"Why did you hate being touched so much anyway?"

I stiffen, but manage to rasp out, "It was the idea of having no control over whose hands were on my body. Touching for me related back to losing control, and I hated it. I hated not being able to stop it. I hated how it felt. The very idea of even fucking had my body coiling so tightly I couldn't breathe. Macy was amazing for that. She taught me that sex, at least, could be more than a horrible feeling. That it could be . . . calming."

Jess wrinkles her nose. "Calming?"

"Sex can be beautiful, Jess."

She smiles. God, she's fucking gorgeous. "No, Dimi. Sex is only beautiful with someone you really, really want it with. Otherwise it's just fucking."

"Maybe, honey," I murmur. "But it was my medicine for a long time."

She nods and stares down at her hands.

"But you should never do it if it isn't what you really want."

She snaps her head up and looks me right in the eye. "I can't hide forever, Dimi. I want it and, more than anything, I want it with you."

"You askin' me to make love to you, baby?" I grin.

She flushes and shakes her head. "No, I'm asking you to fuck me."

I raise my brows. "Fuck you?"

"Yes," she whispers. "Fuck me. I want to feel that raw passion. I want to feel the heat that sparks inside me when I'm around you. Maybe next time you can make love to me."

"There'll be a next time?"

She looks at me as though I'm stupid. "Of course, Dimi."

Well fuck.

She's killing me . . . in the best possible way.

~

Jess

I'm terrified, yet everything inside me is ready, including my heart. What happened to me when I was younger was less than desirable and it scarred a huge part of me, but now has come the time when

I can either let it consume me, or deal with it and move on. I don't want to spend my life without a man. I trust Dimi, for whatever reason, and I know he wouldn't hurt me. He's the only person I have ever wanted this from and my decision is clear.

Dimi pulls me closer to him, pressing his hard body against mine. He shifts to the side just slightly and grips my chin, turning it so he can press his forehead against mine. We sit like that for a long, long few minutes, just breathing each other in. Then, finally, his hands start moving up my thigh. I'm in only a towel, so there's nothing stopping him from inching farther. I take a deep, steadying breath and watch his fingers disappear under my towel.

"Dimi?" I whisper.

"Mmmm," he murmurs, nuzzling his nose into my neck.

"I'm scared."

He stops his hand immediately and pulls back, looking me in the eye.

"If there's ever a second you can't take it, or you find it's too much, you tell me to stop. I swear to you, Jess, I will stop. I won't ever, *ever* hurt you."

I believe him, I really do.

"I trust you."

His eyes widen and a deep warmth fills their depths. I'm guessing that's not something he's heard a lot in his life, and I certainly don't think he's ever had someone put so much in his hands. I reach up and stroke the light stubble on his cheek, before pulling him close to me and kissing him. It starts off slow and sweet, but quickly turns deep and intense.

His fingers slide up higher as the kiss turns scorching. I don't know what I want to feel the most—his tongue dancing with mine or the way his fingers graze my naked sex. He doesn't press in, he just delivers feather-light touches up and down my pussy, not yet taking that plunge. I groan into his mouth and push my hips forward, needing to feel him, needing to ease the throbbing ache that's slowly intensifying between my legs.

"Dimi," I gasp. "Please."

He gently slips his finger into my depths, finding my aching clit. I love the feeling. Pleasure shoots up my spine and causes tingles to break out over my skin. Dimitri's finger slides gently over my hardening nub, tweaking it until I'm squirming, needing more. He presses a hand to my chest and gently lays me down, and my towel slips off. The cool air tickles my skin, causing a gasp to escape my lips.

He's torturing me; I know it. He moves down so he's kneeling, and he gently plants kisses from my feet up to my thigh. My skin tingles as his mouth moves over my skin. Every now and then he slides his tongue out, creating little circles. I shiver, my nipples hard and my pussy aching as he finds my cleft. He pushes his tongue through my wet folds, and I moan and arch, before he slowly lets me go and trails kisses up my belly.

"That was mean," I breathe.

He chuckles. "It has to be worth it. I might try that again."

He kisses me softly, before moving back down so he's kneeling on the bed, and he slowly spreads my legs once more. He runs a finger up and down my damp sex as he gently parts my folds. He sucks in a breath and murmurs something under his breath that sounds like "Holy fuck." I squirm as he begins massaging my clit again.

"Dimi," I cry out.

He swirls his fingertip around and around until I'm arching, calling his name. Then very gently and very slowly, he slides a finger into my pussy. I buck my hips, shocked by the overwhelming pleasure I'm experiencing now. Dimitri curls his finger, finding a spot that has his name stumbling off my tongue over and over. He strokes it until I'm hanging on the edge, then suddenly he stops.

"The first time you come, baby, it's going to be around my cock."

I make a pained protest but that's quickly cut off when he stands up, fully naked and erect. Oh. My. God. I stare at his cock, fascinated. He reaches down, wrapping a hand around it and stroking it up and down. My entire body breaks out into tiny goose bumps, and I find myself biting my bottom lip so hard I taste blood. Holy shit, he's perfect. He continues stroking as he reaches down to his pants and rifles through them until he finds a condom.

I watch as he rips the packet open with his teeth and then rolls it down his impressive length. Then he crawls back onto the bed. "How do you want this, baby?"

I shake my head, confused. "I-I . . . don't know?"

"Me on top, you on top, on the side, back to front . . ."

I gape at him. "W-w-what?"

"Baby," he chuckles. "How do you want it?"

I bite my lip again, wincing when I feel the sensitive spot I've created.

"You on top."

He grins and crawls toward me, meeting me with his lips to mine. He kisses me and slowly lowers me onto the bed, shifting between my legs. I wrap one leg around his hip and leave the other hitched up by his side. He kisses down my neck and his hands gently tweak my nipples. I feel him pressing against my opening and I clench my eyes shut, feeling my breathing deepen.

"Look at me, Jess."

I open my eyes and look into his.

"Don't turn your eyes from me."

I stare into his blue depths as he slowly pushes forward. I grit my teeth as a full, slightly painful sensation radiates through my body. He strokes my cheek, using one hand to prop himself up as he continues inching inside me. The moment the pain subsides and he's fully inside me, I realize just how beautiful this can be. I don't realize I've been holding my breath until it comes out in a whoosh.

Dimitri presses his forehead against mine and gently pulls out before slowly pushing back in. I gasp and squirm beneath him. He's being gentle, and it's amazing, but I want him to consume me, to ravish me, to take my breath away. I reach up, pressing my fingernails into his back. He flinches and stiffens.

"You don't like that?" I whisper between pants.

He grinds his jaw and shakes his head. I lower my hands, placing them back by my sides.

"Here," he rasps, slapping his biceps. "Touch here."

I lift my hands again, curling my fingers around his bulging biceps. His muscles flex underneath my fingertips and he jerks his hips out, pushing back in a little harder this time. His cock swells inside me; I can feel every inch of him.

"Dimi," I plead. "Faster."

He begins thrusting harder, rotating his hips in *that* way. I feel the pressure building deep in my core. A strangled moan escapes my lips when he leans down and bites my neck. I arch my back, pressing my breasts to his chest. The feeling of his skin rubbing against my nipples has the pleasure building higher and higher.

"D-D-Dimi . . ." I gasp.

"On it, baby," he growls. "Hang tight."

He thrusts harder, deeper, until I'm shuddering beneath him and hanging on the edge. His jaw is tight and his eyes are closed as his entire body stiffens for its release.

"I . . ." Oh God, the pleasure. "Now, Dimi."

A burst of something beautiful releases and shoots through my body, causing everything inside me to feel as though it's slowly exploding in the most amazing, intense way. I scream out Dimi's name and my nails slide down his biceps. He groans low and deep in his throat and then I feel him swell inside me before he, too, finds his earth-shattering explosion.

When we both come down from our high, Dimitri slumps over, holding himself up only just slightly with his left hand pressed flat to the bed. He drops his mouth to my neck and slowly runs his tongue up, causing another shudder to leave my body. Then he pulls out and rolls, pulling me onto my side. His face nuzzles into my hair and his arms wrap around my body.

That was perfect; it was everything my first time should have been. I'd missed out on that kind of passion before now, but he made it up to me, he made sure it was as perfect as it could be. I tangle my fingers into his and bring our joined hands to my lips, kissing his fingertips. He runs his fingers up and down my side, causing me to tingle all over.

"You okay?" he murmurs against my ear.

I giggle softly at the contact. "Mmmm."

"Is that a good mmmm, or a bad mmmm?"

"I didn't know there was such a thing as a bad mmmm."

He chuckles throatily. "A bad mmmm is one you get when you're disappointed or angry and you have no words. So when someone asks you something, you just give them an mmmm."

"Oh," I laugh softly. "Then it's a good mmmm."

"Really?"

I roll my eyes even though he can't see it. "What did you think I would say?"

He strokes his fingers down to my thigh and back up again. "No smart Jess remark?"

"Hey," I mumble. "I can be serious."

"I know, baby," he whispers, nipping my earlobe.

"Stop being so sweet, it doesn't suit you."

He laughs. "That makes two of us that aren't behaving."

"Truth," I yawn.

We lay in silence for the longest moment and I feel my eyelids beginning to droop. Just as I'm about to drift off, Dimitri mutters, "Where is he, Jess?"

I blink a few times, but my eyes are so heavy I can't force them open. So, I just let them stay closed, but I answer him anyway. "Who?"

"Hendrix."

That has my eyes flicking open. "Dimi . . ."

"I need to see him, no matter what you think, no matter what he wants. I have to see him to get this closure."

"I don't know if I trust that you won't hurt him."

"Neither do I," he says, his voice heavy with regret. "But I can't ever be truly complete until I see him."

I close my eyes again, sighing deeply. "Would you hear him out? Would you let him tell his side? Or would you just kill him?"

"For the sake of not losing you, Jess, I'd hear him out."

"Can you promise me that?"

He pulls me tighter. "A simple yes or no won't be enough. So I'm goin' to put this the best way I can. You've been through a lot, possibly even worse than what I lived through, so you understand something about me that no one has ever understood. You understand fear, pain, hesitation and loss. You understand how hard it is to give someone your trust, and you understand that you cherish the few you do trust because they're likely to be all you'll ever have. I can't promise you not to have a reaction, Jess, because unless I'm a hundred percent sure, I don't give promises. But I can promise you this—I will give you what you need, I will hear him out, because you're one of the few people I've trusted in such a long time and I'm not going to give that up."

I feel a tear trickle down my cheek and I struggle to take a calming breath. He's told me everything I've needed to hear for so long. His finger slides up and swipes the tear. I don't even know how he guessed it was there.

"I can call him," I whisper. "I can organize something."

I feel him exhale. "Thank you."

"But if you hurt him, Dimi . . . I don't . . . I don't—"

"I know," he cuts me off. "I know, Jess."

I nod. "You're right, I do understand a lot of things about you because I'm the same, so I understand trusting very few people. I'm giving you my trust, Dimitri. Please don't crush it. I don't give it back easily."

"Noted," he murmurs.

I hope I'm making the right choice.

CHAPTER TWENTY-ONE

Jess

"Hey, it's me," I say, tucking my legs underneath me on the seat. "Jessie," Hendrix murmurs like he's just woken up.

"Did I wake you?"

He yawns. "No."

"Such a liar." I laugh weakly.

"Somethin' wrong?" he asks.

I stare out at the beautiful row of trees at the base of the yard. It's a cool morning and I'm enjoying the fresh air that's washing through and tickling my skin.

"Dimitri found out we saw each other."

"Shit," he says, his voice filling with emotion. "Jessie, are you hurt? Did he hurt you?"

"No, I'm okay."

"What happened?"

I swallow and take a deep breath. "He wants to see you, Hendrix."

He sighs. "Is that a good idea?"

I honestly don't know.

"He promised to hear you out . . . it's the best I've got. I can't tell you if he'll attack or if he won't but he needs this as much as you do."

"Give me a bit of time to think on it, Jessie, yeah?"

I nod. "Yeah, okay."

"Look, Indi is beside me tugging the fuck outta my pants because she wants to speak with you."

"Your pants?" I ask with my brows raised.

"Got no shirt on," he chuckles.

"Such a rebel she is," I smile. "Throw her on."

"I'll call you on this number in a few days, Jessie."

"Okay."

"Puttin' Indi on."

God, here goes.

~

Dimitri

I lean against the doorframe and watch her curled up on the chair outside. She's got the phone pressed to her ear and she's smiling. A real beautiful smile. I can't bring myself to interrupt. Seeing her like this, it warms something inside me.

"Hey, Indi," she says.

I tilt my head and listen. She slaps a hand over her mouth and smothers a giggle.

"I know," she begins before she's clearly cut off. A giggle finally breaks free and the sound is goddamned beautiful.

"Indigo, shut your pie hole for a second . . ."

I grin, I can't help it.

"I am not 'banging' the enemy . . ."

She laughs again.

"Okay, well, I am, but . . ."

I feel my grin get bigger.

"INDI!" she shouts. "Do you hear this laughter?"

I stop smiling and listen closer, taking a step out.

"Yes, that's real laughter. He makes me laugh. Laughter isn't something I have a whole lot of, but he gives it to me."

Silence.

"Yes," she whispers. "I think . . . I think he could make me happy."

Something burns in my chest. Something deep and consuming.

"I'll call you again soon, I swear."

She smiles and swipes a tear from her cheek.

"Sure, okay."

She waits a second.

"Hey," she says and I feel my body stiffen. Is it him she's talking to now?

"Okay," she begins and then stops. "Yeah, okay. Thank you, Hendrix. I . . . I miss you."

There goes my chest again.

"He's good. It's good. Call me as soon as you can."

I drop my head, taking a deep breath.

"Okay. Bye."

She turns the phone off and lets out a deep, emotional sigh. Then she turns and sees me standing at the door. There's something about her face, I can't quite pinpoint what it is. Her cheeks are rosy and her eyes are sparkling. Those people, they bring out a beauty in her. They make her happy. They make her whole. It's written all over her.

"Hey," she whispers and then holds the phone up. "I called Hendrix."

"I heard," I say, walking out.

"He's going to call me as soon as he can."

I nod and grab a chair, spinning it around and sitting on it, pressing the back of it to my chest. I rest my chin on it and stare at her.

"You good?"

She nods, and her cheeks pinken just slightly.

"I'm good."

"Hungry?"

She nods.

I grin.

Fuck, this girl is consuming me. For the first time in my entire time of seeking revenge, I woke up without thinking about killing him.

CHAPTER TWENTY-TWO

Jess

"God," I groan, rubbing my belly. "I'm so full."

"You ate more than me," Dimitri grins.

"I was hungry."

"Sure you ain't a man beneath all that beauty?"

"Well," I say, leaning back to ease the pressure in my belly. "I can't be entirely sure . . . I mean there was that secret operation when I was a baby."

"Ha ha," he smirks. "Your pussy is too nice to have ever been a dick."

I shake my head and get up, walking over and sitting on the large, soft couch. Dimitri gets up, coffee in hand, and joins me. I shuffle closer to him and sigh.

"Is this for real?"

He puts his arm around my shoulders. "Yeah, baby, I think it is."

I smile and close my eyes, leaning my head against his shoulder.

"Do you remember them?"

"Huh?" I ask, not understanding his question.

"Your parents, do you remember them?"

I smile, but it's a sad one. "Not really, but I do remember some things."

"Tell me?"

"My dad was really happy. The funny kind of happy. I remember he always told me jokes. My momma was beautiful. I recall loving her long, red hair. I used to spend hours brushing it, because I just loved how it felt against my fingers. Each night when I would sleep, they would sing to me, this one song I still remember even after all these years."

"What was it?"

I flush. "I can't sing it."

"Why not?"

"Because I can't sing."

"I wouldn't know, I've never heard it."

I laugh softly. "Be thankful. I've heard geese that sound prettier."

He chuckles. "Go on, Jess. Sing."

"Fine, but if you laugh, I'll stab you."

He doesn't answer, but I feel his chest tremble with laughter. I close my eyes and remember the song my parents used to sing. It was a rhyme that was in a children's book we read once.

"Little Sir Echo, how do you do? Hello . . . Hello. Little Sir Echo, I'm very blue. Hello . . . Hello. Hello. Hello. Won't you come over and play? You're a nice little fellow, I know by your voice, but you're always so far away."

I finish singing and a lump forms in my throat. Dimitri places a hand on the back of my neck and gives it a light squeeze, letting me know he's still there and everything is okay.

"I told you," I croak. "A goose."

"Prettiest fuckin' goose I ever heard."

Pretty sure I just fell in love with him in that tiny second. God help me.

~

"God, Dimi," I gasp, feeling my back ram against the cold brick wall.

Dimitri's hands are on my ass, and his fingers are digging into my flesh. He's using me as leverage for his thrusts. His cock is driving deep, hard and fast. His groans are throaty and the sound has everything clenching inside me in the best possible way. My hands are wrapped around his biceps; my shirt is jacked up exposing my breasts. Every now and then he leans down and sucks one of my nipples into his mouth.

"So fuckin' good around my cock," he groans. "So fuckin' good."

"Dimitri!"

We hear Luke's voice coming through the door. We're outside the house and around the corner against the wall. The door is closed but obviously Luke can come right out.

"Fuck off," Dimitri growls.

"It's urgent. I need you here now."

Dimitri thrusts harder, faster, bringing me closer to the edge. I cry out and his hand quickly leaves my hip and presses against my mouth as he drives me higher and higher. Our skin is slapping together; we're both panting and sweating. I'm going to come so hard, I can feel it in every inch of my body.

When I get there, I throw my head back and scream into Dimitri's hand, clenching around him, feeling my own arousal coat his cock so he is able to move harder and faster to his own release. With a shudder and a throaty moan, he follows close behind me, pulsing hard and deep. When we've stopped panting, he slowly lifts me off him, placing me with care back on my feet.

I wobble but I manage to keep myself upright. I pull my top down and straighten my skirt and panties. It was literally a quick fuck. He looked at me, I looked at him, we started kissing and the next thing I knew he had his jeans down, my panties torn aside, and we were fucking, hard and sweet. Dimitri pulls the condom off and ties it, before shoving it into his pocket.

Mega ew.

"Gotta go deal with Luke," he rasps, his voice still croaky.

"O-okay," I whisper, unable to find mine.

He grins at me and turns, walking off while buttoning up his jeans. God, he's beautiful. I watch him go with a smile on my face and a sweet-ass swell between my legs.

I'm almost sure it doesn't get better than this.

~

"I hate you fighting," I say, running my hand over his ass as I pass him.

"Yeah," he chuckles. "I know."

"Can't you just drug your opponent and run off, living happily ever after?"

He laughs loudly. "No, baby, that's not how it works."

"What if he beats you?"

He gives me a look while strapping his hands. "He won't."

"Dimitri, you don't know that."

"I do know that."

"Such an arrogant ass," I mumble under my breath.

He reaches over, nudging my cheek gently with his bound fist. "Stop being a baby."

I shove my fist into his cheek. "Stop being an arrogant ass."

"Deal."

He turns and takes hold of his shirt, yanking it off.

"It's really not a wonder girls come to these fights," I say, crossing my arms and admiring his sculpted, beautiful back.

"And why is that?"

"You have a nice ass. So do half the other fighters."

He turns and gives me an intense expression. "You lookin' at the other fighters?"

I grin at him and uncross my arms, tapping my chin as if I'm thinking. "Well, there was that one . . . he had this ass to die for. I wanted to jump into the ring and—"

Dimitri lunges forward, wrapping his arm around my waist and hauling me up close to his body.

"Only man you jump in the ring for is me," he murmurs, staring at my lips. Then he leans forward and places a smacking kiss against them.

"Yes, boss," I breathe.

"Now, go and find Luke, we need to get this fight started."

I pout but nod. I turn and head toward the door just as it opens and Luke walks in, followed by Malibu. I sigh and roll my eyes as she lets her gaze travel over Dimitri. She walks past me as if I don't exist and heads straight over to Dimi. She puts her hands on his arms and grins at him.

"Dimi," she murmurs.

He takes her hands and peels her fingers off his arms. "Not interested."

She stares at him, shocked. "What?"

"You heard me. Now, out, I have a fight."

"She's in here," she snaps, jerking her head toward me.

"She's my girl, she's allowed in here."

Her face tightens and she turns, glaring at me. "Well," she grates out. "I guess that answers that then."

"If you're watchin' the fight, then go and sit down," Dimi says to her. "But you know you're not allowed in here."

"I hate being out there alone, it scares me. She can come with me."

She actually does look like it bothers her, and I feel kind of bad about that. There are a lot of people out there that are less than desirable.

"I'll go with you, but if you so much as say one bad word to me, I'll drop you into the middle of a group of horny men and let them do what they may."

She glowers at me. "You'd better watch your mouth."

I raise my brows, crossing my arms. "Or what?"

"Enough!" Dimitri says. "Luke, take the girls out. I'll get Josh in here to help me."

"Who's Josh?" I ask.

"The manager of this place. We're tight," Dimi says, staring at me.

"Fine," Malibu mutters.

"Whatever," I say.

Luke sighs.

Dimitri walks over, taking my face and pressing a sizzling kiss to my lips. "Cheer for me, baby."

Oh I will.

I'll cheer my little heart out.

CHAPTER TWENTY-THREE

Jess

I'm transfixed—my eyes are stuck to the sweating, pulsing man in front of me. God, when Dimitri fights, I forget everything else around me. The room goes out of focus and all I can see is him. His fists swinging, his body flexing and moving, the determined look on his face. My cheeks flush as I recall how my mouth has been on that body. I tremble and rub my arms, trying to keep the goose bumps at bay.

"Jessica!"

I jerk and turn my head to see Malibu staring at me, her expression annoyed.

"What?"

"I've been calling you!"

I roll my eyes. "I was watching. What do you want?"

"I need to go to the bathroom and I don't want to go alone. These places freak me out."

I grumble in annoyance. I have to take her. There is no way Luke will leave me to take her to the toilet, which means I'm the only one who can go with her. I shove to my feet and glare down at her. "Well, hurry up."

"Bossy," she mutters, getting to her feet.

Luke leans forward and whispers into my ear. "Where are you goin'?"

"Toilet, because Barbie can't seem to go on her own."

"What did you call me?" Malibu mutters, crossing her arms.

"Nothing," I reply, smiling sweetly.

She mumbles something under her breath as I turn back to Luke. "We'll be no more than five minutes."

He nods. "Be careful."

I smile. There are a few reasons why. The first is that Luke is letting me go alone, which means Dimi trusts me. The second is that Luke now trusts me too. Keeping my smile, I trek forward, shoving through people to try to make my way to the toilets at the back. The entire time I'm focusing on getting through people, Malibu is complaining because people keeping "grabbing" her ass. We reach the toilets only to see a fifty-person line-up.

"You've got to be kidding me!" Malibu snaps, then grabs my arm. "Come on, we'll use the staff ones out back."

I don't bother to argue; I figure she's been to enough fights with Dimi to know where the toilets are in the different locations. So, I let her drag me out back. We go through an old, cracked wooden door that leads out onto a dimly lit patio. There are cars lined up to the left and I can hear the traffic to the right. I'm guessing this is the staff car park.

"Come on," Malibu says, leading me toward a set of two doors.

We're just about there when I hear the sound of crunching boots. "Finally," Malibu mutters, spinning us around. I'm confused for a second, unsure what she's talking about. I can't see anyone around, though I can still hear the boots. I also notice that she's not yet let go of my hand.

"Good job, Livvie," I hear a voice say.

Suddenly six men step out of the darkness and into the dull light. My heart stops beating. Roger is the man leading, and he's got a smile on his face that tells me this isn't a coincidence. My heart jerks to life and I try to tug my hand from Malibu's but she's not letting me go. I spin around, kicking my foot out and connecting with her shins. She screams and drops my hand, stumbling a few steps back. I launch forward, but I don't get far before Roger has his hand wrapped around my arm, hauling me back.

I can't scream because his other hand quickly goes over my mouth while two of his men pin my arms. I squirm, but it's no use. The men are too strong and there are too many of them. Tears well in my eyes and I struggle to breathe as I realize the situation I've just been put in. She set me up. She knew they were going to be here tonight. She had this all planned. That's why it doesn't surprise me when one of the men steps forward with an envelope.

"Five thousand dollars, as promised," Roger says, and I can feel his breath near my ear.

I gag behind his hand, which only makes him laugh. I watch in horror as Malibu opens the envelope and counts the money, before looking up with a grin. "Enjoy her."

"Make sure Dimitri thinks she's run off."

No. Oh no. If Dimitri thinks I've run . . . oh . . . God. No . . . He won't believe her. We've shared so much, he'll hesitate, he'll figure out something is wrong. He will. I begin to rattle, my knees turning to jelly. My body slumps and tears tumble down my cheeks as I make eye contact with Malibu.

"Sorry," she mutters. "But you're nothing more than a thorn in my side. I did what I had to."

She turns to Roger. "He won't believe I let her just run, so you need to make it look real."

"With pleasure," Roger mutters, letting go of my mouth and shoving me into another man's arms.

"He'll kill you for this!" I scream.

Another hand clamps over my mouth, and Malibu doesn't seem affected by my words. No, she's not, because she's concentrating on Roger. She closes her eyes and scrunches her face up. What is she doing? I'm staring at her in confusion when Roger's fist lashes out and connects with her eye. She screams and stumbles backwards, falling in the dirt, only adding to the effect.

"Pleasure doing business with you," Roger says, turning back to me. "Time for revenge, Blair."

I scream under the other man's hand and squirm as hard as I can. It's futile. Roger steps forward, extracting a needle from his pocket.

"Sleepy time."

He jabs it into my neck seconds before everything goes black.

~

Dimitri

My eyes scan the crowd after my fight, but I can't see her. Luke is staring around now too, looking a little concerned. I leap off the stage and shove through the grabbing hands and raving fans until I reach him. I take hold of his arm and spin him around. "Where is she?"

He looks confused. "They went to the toilet."

"They?"

"Her and Livvie."

I turn and start shoving my way through the crowd in the direction of the toilets. I haven't got halfway there when Livvie appears. Her face is bloody, she's wild with anger, and she's covered in dirt.

"What the fuck?" I growl, taking her arm. "Where's Jess?"

"How should I know?" she screams. "She punched me the minute we got outside to the toilet and ran. She fucking ruined my shoes."

"What do you mean she ran?" I growl. "And why the fuck were you outside?"

"The toilets inside were too full, so we went to the staff ones. The minute we got out there she turned, said sorry, and punched me so hard I went ass up. Then she bolted."

Bolted.

She bolted.

My chest seizes. Jess ran. She took a chance and she ran. All along, all the feelings, it's all been just a way to gain my trust. My vision blurs and I find my fingers tightening on Livvie's arm.

"Shit, Dimi, stop it. You're hurting me."

"Where. The. Fuck. Did. She. Go?" I grate out, my voice icy.

"How the hell should I know? She just ran toward the street."

I spin, taking Livvie with me. I turn to Luke and shove her at him. "Take her. I've got to find Jess."

He looks concerned. "Where'd she go?"

"She ran."

His face pales. "Shit, boss, sorry. I thought . . . I thought she wanted to be here. The way she was watchin' you. Fuck, I'm sorry."

"She's played us all," I grind out, feeling my hands tremble with rage. "But she won't win. I'll find her, Luke. I know exactly where she will have gone."

He looks right into my eyes. "Load the ship?"

"Load the fuckin' ship," I growl. "We're goin' to sea."

CHAPTER TWENTY-FOUR

Jess

My head pounds as I slowly open my eyes. I can't see anything for a moment, everything seems to be blurred shapes. I go to reach up and rub my eyes, only to feel that I'm shackled. My heart begins to pound and I blink as rapidly as I can to clear my vision. When it clears enough for me to take in my surrounds, I see that I'm in a tiny cell. It's not bigger than two meters by two meters. I can only just lie down in it. There's a tiny, old mattress, which I'm on, and nothing else.

No windows.

Nothing.

I sit up frantically and jerk at the cuffs. They're tight—so tight that if I'm not careful, and I rattle them too much, they'll get tighter and stop the blood flowing into my hand. I realize when I move my feet that they're cuffed too. I'm connected to a large shackle in the stone wall. Sweat breaks out across my skin and I swallow, trying to ease my dry throat. I try not to let fear in, but there's no way of stopping it.

My nightmare has found me.

I let more tears leak out. They burn my eyes. Roger has me, there's no turning back from him. He's got me and Dimitri doesn't know where I am. Worse, he thinks I've run from him. Which means he's not going to look for me. A sick feeling swells in my stomach and I feel myself begin to shake with panic. This could likely be where my road ends. In a cell, being tortured by a man who should be dead.

I drop my head and sob.

My sobbing comes to a halt when the cell door rattles. I jerk my head up and push myself up against the wall. Fear swells in my body as I stare, transfixed, waiting to see who will come in. The moment I see Roger, everything turns from fear to something so much more. Something so intense I forget to breathe. He smiles at me, satisfied, gloating.

"Well, I bet you never thought you'd be here, did you, Blair?"

"What do you want from me?" I croak. It's a stupid question, though. I know exactly what he wants from me—revenge.

"You know, I thought of many ways over the years that I could make you pay. I thought it would be fun to just kill you. Then I figured I'd rape you because, let's face it, that's where this all started." He grins at me and I lean over and dry retch. "But that all seemed so . . . cliché. So, I came up with something better. Something that allows me to watch you suffer, all the while making me money."

I lift my tear-blurred vision and stare at him, confused.

"I can't tell you right now, but you'll find out more tonight when I put you to the test. Of course, if my plan is ineffective, I'll simply kill you."

God, please help me.

"I'll leave you with that, shall I?"

"You're a monster," I growl, my voice pathetic and low.

He throws his head back and laughs, causing strands of wispy gray to flow around his shoulders. When he's finished laughing, he lowers his head and stares me dead in the eyes. "You haven't seen the worst of me yet, Blair. You'll pay for what you did to my face, pay for the years I spent getting taunted, pay for everything you did to make my life hell."

"Your life!" I growl. "What about what you did to mine?"

"I was teaching you a lesson. You should have taken it instead of being ungrateful."

"A lesson." I laugh bitterly. "Is that what you call it? I'd love to know how ripping my innocence from me at such a young age was considered a lesson."

He smirks at me. "I got you ready for other men, so when you had a husband he could appreciate a well-fucked woman."

"A woman!" I scream, jerking on my chains and thrashing my body. "I was a fucking kid. A child!"

He shrugs. "Child, woman, same parts, same feeling."

I jerk so hard the cuffs burn into my wrists. I scream so loudly my voice cracks and I can hear no more than a strangled gasp. He laughs again, stepping forward and leaning down. He takes my hair in his hands and yanks me forward. My hair feels like it is ripping out of my scalp.

"Felt nice, too. Fucking you slowly, listening to you scream—"

"Die!" I wail. "You piece of shit!"

He chuckles as he turns. "I'm done here. Be ready for tonight. It's a live or die kind of situation."

He exits the room without another word.

I want to curl up and die.

~

Dimitri

"Have you found the phone?" I ask, storming into Luke's room on the ship.

He's standing at his desk, but at the sound of my voice he turns and stares at me, his expression compassionate. Fuck compassion.

I don't want compassion. I just want to fucking find her and show her that I'm not the kind of person she fucks with.

"No," Luke says, his voice weary.

"Fuck!" I bellow. "How am I supposed to find him?"

"You've got the recourses, Dimitri. Just go back through what you've got."

"It's not enough!" I bellow. "We couldn't fuckin' find him last time."

"He's not going to hide now," he adds. "He's going to be waiting because he knows Jess is safe now that she's with him. He's got no reason to hide from you."

"This is fucked up," I growl, running my hands through my hair. "She completely fucked me over."

"I'm sorry about that, boss."

I turn and walk out of the room, not saying another word. What is there to say? She used me. She made me think that I could finally trust someone, that maybe my need for revenge was dramatic and misinformed. It was all a lie. She was never interested in helping me; she was only luring me close enough so she could get the chance to run. The moment she got that chance, she took it.

Now who's the fool?

That's what you get for trusting.

CHAPTER TWENTY-FIVE

Jess

L et me go!" I cry as Roger drags me down a set of rickety stairs. We seem to be going underground. The stairs are going lower and lower and it's getting darker and smellier down here. As we draw closer, I can hear the sounds of chattering voices. Other people? Why would he take me in front of other people? He reaches a large, metal door and shoves it open, dragging me into a well-lit room. I gape when I see what he's got down here.

A fighting ring.

There's a massive ring in the middle, surrounded by a floor to ceiling cage. My stomach turns and I struggle to keep the vomit from rising. Why would he make people fight in a cage? As we move closer, I notice the ten or so people in the room have stopped speaking. I can feel their eyes on me, burning into the back of my head as I move. I keep my eyes to the floor as Roger pulls me closer to the ring.

He's not going to make me fight . . . is he?

Suddenly I'm sure I can't keep the vomit down. I begin to retch. Roger spins me around in front of him and slaps my face hard. I cry out, cupping my cheek. "Stop your fuckin' retching. I need you in top form."

Top form?

"Rex," a man says, approaching Roger.

It clicks now. Rex is obviously his name in this world.

"How are we doin', Trev?"

"Ready to go. Sheila is raring. This your girl?"

The man's eyes turn to me and look me up and down. "She ain't big enough, Rex. She'll get knocked down in one hit."

Oh God.

Oh no.

My knees begin to tremble and my skin prickles all over.

"We'll give her a go. Sometimes the smallest fighters are in fact the best."

The man looks unconvinced, but nods anyway. He turns and disappears, muttering something about five minutes. Then Roger turns to me, smirking. "Ready to fight, little Blair?"

"What?" I gasp, feeling my bottom lip tremble.

"I have big plans for you, but I need to see how you move. If you succeed, you'll be doing this . . . shall we say . . . more regularly?"

No.

"I can't f-f-f-fight."

"Oh, but you can. I know all about where you've been all these years. Don't try to tell me you don't know what you're doing."

"I don't know where you got your information," I rasp. "But it's wrong."

He grins and looks down at me, bringing his face closer. "So you haven't been on a ship with pirates, all of whom are run by a man named Hendrix?"

My knees give way. I fall to the ground and he lets me go, staring down at me as if I'm some sort of pathetic loser. He doesn't jerk me up, he just leans over me and begins to taunt.

"I know you're pathetic, but you've got only two choices here, Blair. You fight and you come away unscathed, or you don't fight and you get beaten to within an inch of your life. You decide."

"You'll kill me," I cry, trembling.

"Then you will fight."

No, he can't do this to me. I'm not a fighter. I've spent my life trying to be anything but. I can't be what he wants me to be.

"Sheila's ready," someone yells.

I turn my eyes to the ring to see a large, raven-haired girl jumping from side to side, just like Dimitri does. I begin to shake all over. She's twice the size of me and she looks like she wants to snarl and rip apart the next thing that comes close. That thing is me. Roger reaches down, jerking me to my feet. "If you don't want her to kill you, fight."

He drags me toward the ring. No . . . no. I struggle, kicking and screaming as loudly as I can. Nobody notices—well, more to the point, nobody cares. They're all here to see if I'm going to be good enough to make them money. They won't get money from me. I'd rather die. Wouldn't I?

When we reach the ring, Roger shoves me in and my world clouds over. I can't see, I can't think, I can't fucking breathe. I see a pair of blue eyes in my head and I tell myself over and over that he'll come for me. He won't let me die. He won't let me stay here . . . he won't. He'll fight for me.

The raven-haired girl glares at me, and my skin prickles. I struggle to fight back the tears welling in my eyes. I can't let her see my fear but how do I hide it? How do I pretend that the entire situation doesn't scare me. I can't. She knows she's got me, and she is smiling about it. A crooked grin that most definitely tells me she's going to enjoy every single hit.

"One!" someone yells.

My eyes dart around, and I feel panic swell in my chest. I can't fight. I don't know how.

"Two!"

Please, no. Don't let this be—

"Three!"

Suddenly she lunges toward me, only seconds after the man has stopped counting. I step quickly to the left automatically, but it doesn't save me—no, it doesn't even deter her. She swings and her fist connects with my jaw, sending me spiraling around in a full three sixty. I don't scream, I can't. My jaw feels as though it's dislocated. Tears burn in my eyelids.

I feel her hand curl around my hair and tug, nearly ripping it from my scalp. She brings her foot up and puts it against my back, pushing it so hard my spine cracks and I arch forward, going down on my knees unwillingly. I hear the people screaming and yelling for her to "beat the fuck" out of me. I've no hope—she's so strong and I'm so broken.

When her foot comes down over my spine, I finally scream. Pain shoots up my back and travels right down my arms and legs. Her foot connects with my ribs and I roll, trying hard to protect myself from ending up with broken bones. It doesn't protect my face—her foot hits my nose so hard I see stars. I can no longer hear my own screaming as blood spurts from my nose and lands on the floor. Then it travels quickly down my face and fills my mouth until I'm choking on it.

"Enough!" Roger roars.

I don't hear anything more, because my entire world goes black.

CHAPTER TWENTY-SIX

Dimitri

W e're picking up a ship!" Luke says, shoving his finger toward the screen.

"Any idea whose it is?" I ask, tapping my fingers impatiently on the wooden desk.

"No, but we've been out here for days. It's the closest thing we've gotten. These are his waters, we can only hope . . ."

"Get the men up on deck, get all the weapons. He's not running from us again."

Luke nods and disappears, and I stare at the screen with the pulsing dot that indicates another ship. I pray that it's her—I need it to be. For days I've sat out here, lost in my thoughts, wondering if everything we shared was all just a big fucking lie. She let me give a piece of myself to her, and she's gone on to crush that piece until now there is nothing left but pure hatred.

I turn and walk out of the office and up onto the deck. I can see a ship in the distance, but it's too small for me to make out if it's him or not. I fuckin' hope it is. I'm tired of searching, tired of fuckin' trying to be something I'm not. I need to sort this with her, tell her how much I hate her. I drop my head. Fuck, I don't hate her, that's the problem. I want to . . . but I don't. She's consumed me.

"Boss, it's them."

My head snaps up and my eyes grow hard. Face to face with two people who have fucked my world. I straighten my shoulders and walk to the side of the ship, just watching Hendrix draw closer. His ship isn't bigger than mine, but he's got more men. I've got more weapons. We all hold up our guns as the ship gets close enough that I can see the men on board. And him. Fuck.

He's got his hands on the railings and he's staring at me. It isn't a glare, and it isn't pleased. It's just a blank stare. He's got a pretty young girl by his side—that must be the girl Jess was talking about. I give her a casual look, and, surprisingly, she smiles at me. Why the fuck would she smile at me? I'm guessing she thinks Jess and me are something special. Surely by now she knows we're not. Considering Jess ran back to them.

"Dimitri! And to what do I owe this visit?" Hendrix says, tilting his head and studying me.

My hands shake, I want to fucking shoot him and yet, at the same time, seeing him warms something inside me. I'm torn. It's all her fucking fault for making me second guess everything I believed in.

"Don't play stupid with me, Hendrix. You know exactly why I'm here."

He shakes his head, having the fucking nerve to look confused. "Actually, I don't."

"I know she's with you, so just hand her over so I can talk to her."

Something in his face changes; he gets a look that has my skin prickling.

"What are you talkin' about?"

I grind my jaw. "Jess, where is she?"

Hendrix straightens and his eyes narrow. "What do you mean where is she? She's with you."

"Don't play fuckin' stupid. I know you're protectin' her and there's no point. Give her up and we can walk away from this unscathed."

He shakes his head. "I don't fucking have her, Dimitri. And you're scaring me."

"Stop lying and just bring her out!" I shout.

"She's not here," the girl by his side whispers.

I turn my eyes to her. If not for the fact that her expression is truly worried, I wouldn't have believed her.

"What do you mean she's not here?"

She shakes her head. "She said she was with you and—"

"She ran!" I yell, lifting my hands and clutching the sides of my head. "I thought she came to you."

Hendrix curses loudly. "She's not fucking here, Dimitri."

My face hardens. If she's not here . . . then where the hell is she?

∼

Jess

I'm freezing cold. My entire body feels like it's slowly turning to ice from the inside out. I've got no blankets, just this crappy mattress. I'm aching all over, it hasn't stopped for days, but like Roger has told me countless times, it could have been worse. I don't know how. How could it get worse than this? The girl beat the living hell out of me, and he let her.

I guess now he is going to see I can't do it. I'm not a fighter.

"Get up."

I lift my head to see Roger at the door. He's glaring at me. I turn away.

"Did you not fucking hear me? Get the fuck up."

I don't answer.

He storms over, leaning down and gripping my arm before hauling me up so hard I lose my footing and fall into him. He shoves me back and begins the insults again. "You're a fucking worthless waste of space. There never was any hope for you. Your parents are probably glad they got killed—you're putting them to shame."

His words burn into my core and I feel myself beginning to pant. Is he right? Am I putting them to shame? Am I letting them down? I'm letting him kill me. I'm not even fighting. My father told me to always believe that I can do whatever I have to. I close my eyes, remembering him.

"Angel, don't you ever let anyone tell you that you're not beautiful," he soothes, stroking my hair.

"She told me I was ugly, Daddy," I cry.

He rubs my shoulders. "No one can make you anything you don't want to be. You're beautiful, and as long as you believe it, then the rest doesn't matter. Don't let your friends make you feel anything less than perfect."

Tears run down my cheeks.

"Worthless," Roger taunts. "Just like I thought. I should just let you fucking die. You're not even worth the effort. You can go and join them and show them your pathetic defeat."

I don't even feel my hand lash out, but it does. It comes soaring up and hits him so hard in the face he stumbles two steps backwards. I see my mother's and father's faces, and how they used to be so proud of me. I'm not ready to let them down. I have only two choices now—fight or die. I'll fight. I'll fight until my last breath because that's how I was taught.

Never give up.

I lunge at Roger even though my body screams at me to stop. I bring my knee up and hit him so hard in the groin he roars in pain. As he drops down, I bring my other knee up into his face. At his cries, two men rush into the room and tackle me until I'm restrained. I'm panting as Roger gets to his feet.

"You're fucking wrong," I growl. "Nothing will stop me."

He grins even though his face is masked with pain.

"I knew it was in there."

"You'll regret this one day," I vow. "I swear it."

He laughs. "Your pirates aren't here to save you this time, princess."

I give him a stare as cold as ice as he straightens and turns to the men holding me back.

"Order me another fight in two days. In the meantime, get me Damon in here."

Damon? Who the hell is Damon?

"On it, boss."

The men let me go and I fall backwards onto the bed. Roger grins at me once more before heading to the door.

"I hope you're ready."

I'll never be ready, but I will fight. I can't die. I'm not finished and the only option I have here is to do as he asks until I can find a way out. Fighting means he's going to take me out in public, which will give me a chance.

CHAPTER TWENTY-SEVEN

Jess

The door opens later that day, and Roger steps inside. He's followed by a man I was not expecting. I knew he was going to bring in this 'Damon' fella, but I didn't realize Damon was a freaking god. I blink a few times as the tall, extremely gorgeous man steps into the room. My mouth opens slightly; it's really hard not to gape. He's got long, thick blond hair and the greenest eyes I've ever seen. He's at least six feet tall and has more muscle than even Dimitri and that's saying something. Dimitri is a big fucking man.

"Damon, this is Blair. Teach her the basics."

Damon turns his eyes to me, and they widen. "You've got to be kidding me, right?"

Roger turns to him with a disgusted expression. "Why would you think I'm kidding?"

"She's tiny, a girl, and I'm not interested."

Roger steps forward and glares at Damon. "She's going to make me a lot of money, therefore you'll get paid well. If you walk out, there will be no money for you and without money, you can't take care of your wife."

Damon flinches. "She's just a fuckin' girl."

"She's run with the best of them for years, she is tougher than she looks."

"I'll teach her the basics, Rex, but that's it."

Roger pats him on the back and he flinches. "Get on it then. Her first fight is in two days."

Damon stares down at me, and with a defeated sigh says, "Get up."

I get to my feet, staring at the huge, gorgeous man in front of me. Roger takes hold of my cuffs and leads me out of the room and back down to the large ring he's got in his basement. He then uncuffs me and clicks his fingers. Six men appear and stand near each window and door in the room. I shake my head with a sigh. Roger turns to Damon.

"Four hours today. Same tomorrow."

Then he turns and leaves the room. Damon gazes at me, his green eyes searching mine.

"What's your name, darlin'?"

I tilt my head. "Huh?"

"You heard me."

"My name is, um . . . Blair."

He stares longer. "What're you doin' here, Blair?"

I hesitate and stare at the guys around. "I . . . well . . . I don't have a choice."

He sighs and rubs his head. "I'm sorry, Blair. I gotta do what I gotta do. The best I can do for you is give you a fighting chance."

My eyes swell with tears. "I understand," I croak.

His face softens but I see his jaw tic. He leans down close. "Is there someone I can get a message to?"

My heart swells with hope.

"Hey!" one of the men barks. "Back up."

Damon stands straight before I can answer him. "Keep your knickers on," he barks at him.

The guy glares at Damon, but eventually turns his focus away. Damon looks back to me and steps closer again, but not close enough to have a quiet conversation.

"For a girl, there are a few basics you need to know when it comes to defending yourself."

I nod, swallowing my tears back.

"You're tiny, but that can be an advantage. Anyone who says a fighter has to be huge is living in a fantasy. You have the chance to duck and hit those sensitive lower parts. You can duck away from a punch much easier than most. That's what we're going to focus on."

He puts his hands on my shoulders and whispers. "The contact, get it to me."

I nod.

"Right, first things. Spread your legs a bit more. You want a good stance at all times, you can't be losing your footing at a vital time."

I spread my legs a little and he nods.

"You keep your fists up as much as you can unless, of course, you're on the floor."

He takes my fists and raises them in a fighter stance.

"If your opponent is bigger than you—which I imagine most will be—don't let it put you off. Focus on what's in front of you. If you can easily hit a stomach, or ribs, or, hell, a pelvis, then do it."

I nod again, feeling my heart thudding.

"So," he says, holding my fists in his large hands. "Most people are going to go straight for the face, it's almost always the case. You see a fist, you duck. While you're ducking, you go in for whatever you can. Remember this—it hurts just as much for a woman to get a fist to the junk as it does for a man. If you can get a hit there, go for it. The other sensitive place is the breasts—however, more often than not they're taped. Doesn't matter, though, I'd imagine it still hurts like a bastard."

I cringe. It would.

"The next best place is the ribs. When you go for a rib jab, go direct. Don't dance around it."

He takes my fist and brings it to his ribcage. "Right here is the weakest part. Hit it hard and fast. Twice if you can."

He raises my fist to his sternum. "Here is enough to put your opponent in a temporary pain haze. While they're winded, you go in for anything else."

He moves my hand to his throat. "Throat punch—works every time if you can get a clear shot. It will take the breath from their lungs and for a second it will feel like they can't breathe. You hit hard and you make it good. Their hands will automatically go up to their throat—while they're up it's leaving the stomach, groin and legs free. Go for the groin over the stomach, which will cause them to double over. When they're down, put a swift kick to the face to bring them down."

I swallow and drop my head, sighing. "I can't do this, I just . . . I can't hurt someone else."

"Listen to me," he says, lifting my chin and forcing me to look at him. "These girls, they're not going to hold back. The fights he's got planned for you are a fight or die kind of situation. You can't afford to be afraid."

"I didn't ask for any of this . . ."

"No one does," he smiles weakly. "But you gotta do what you can to survive. No matter the situation."

I nod and stand up straighter.

"Now, the most important thing in a fight is watching your opponent. Watch their body, watch the way their eyes focus and their arms flinch. Try to understand which way they're going to hit. Sometimes it's too fast and that's impossible, but you never take your eyes off them."

He lets my hand go and steps back.

"We're going to do some basics. I'll come at you—don't worry, I won't hit you—and you need to give me your best reaction."

He launches his fist toward my face and I try desperately to remember what he said about that. I'm too slow—he bops my cheek softly.

"I can't do this," I panic. "I will die before I get a hit in."

He looks me dead in the eye. "You'll only die if you allow yourself to. You have to be angry, you have to be determined. Do you want to get out of here?"

I make a pained sound and whisper, "More than anything."

"Then you fight and you fight with everything you are. Find it, girl, and use it."

I nod and straighten my shoulders. "Again."

He slowly swings his fist toward my face and I duck just in the last second, pushing my fist out until it hits his abdomen hard. He makes an *oomph*ing sound and I groan as my knuckles ache. He's got abs of steel. I don't stop, though, when he brings a knee up and I duck to the side and swing around to his back, lifting my leg and shoving it into his hip, sending him stumbling forward. He spins around with a grin.

"Yes!"

I beam.

"Again."

I'll do it again. I'll fight until all the breath leaves my body.

CHAPTER TWENTY-EIGHT

Dimitri

"Fuck you, Hendrix," I bark, slamming my fist into his desk.

He glares up at me. "Don't take your temper out on me, boy. You want to make me pay, you do it after we've found her. You care about her at all, you'll keep it the fuck together until she's safe."

I grind my jaw. "I care about her more than you, fucker."

He stands, sliding around the desk and charging toward me. His hand lashes out when he reaches me, and connects with my jaw. I roar in pain and retaliate quickly, slamming my fist into his midsection. He bellows and takes two steps back, but I don't give him a break. My fist swings around and hits him in the side of the head, causing his vision to blur. I know this, because I've been hit in the exact same location. He blinks and swings his fist, hitting me square in the ear. My hearing begins to fade and a loud, piercing squealing sound takes its place.

I sink to the ground, and gather my bearings, before spinning around and launching toward his legs. He goes down hard, taking me with him. We land on the floor with a thump, growling and hissing, spitting curses. "You're a no good son of a bitch," I bellow. "You deserve to fucking pay for everything you did."

"Isn't that what you've been doing?" he roars. "Making me fucking pay?"

"I haven't even begun to give you what it is you deserve."

He flips me onto my back, pressing a hand to my throat. I gasp and struggle, launching my fist into his stomach. He stares down at me, eyes wild. "You've made my life a living fucking hell for this past month. You're not even givin' me a fuckin' chance to speak."

"There's nothing to say," I snarl. "You're a no good piece of shit who ruined my life."

"I didn't fuckin' ruin your life," he barks, pressing his hand in harder. "If you listened for five seconds you would know that."

"I gave you everything," I roar. "Everything. I trusted you. I loved you. You gave me something when I had nothing and you let me down. You fuckin' let me down."

His eyes flash and he lets my neck go, leaning back. I lunge at him again, tackling him to the floor and driving another fist into his face.

"Stop it!"

I hear the sound of a female voice, but I don't stop. I lift my body and bring it down over his, causing a loud *oomph* to leave his mouth. He brings his fists up and over my sides, hitting me furiously. I feel my ribs crack. Fuck. I rear my fist back and bring it down right over his groin. He roars, his face scrunching in pain. I'm panting and blood is filling my mouth. I look up and see his girl, Indi, gaping at us.

"What is wrong with you two?" she screams. "Jess is out there, God knows where, and you two are fighting."

Hendrix glares at me, ignoring her. "Don't you ever tell me you care more about that girl than me. You couldn't possibly know her, in the short time you've had her, the way I know her. I was the one who found her half-naked, covered in blood and completely broken all those years ago. I put her back together. You know only what you see now."

"No," I grind out, clenching my fists. "I see what I am in her, and you're right, I didn't put her back together." I stare down at my trembling fists for a second before looking back at him. "But she put me back together, and that's a connection you will never understand."

"I fuckin' understand, more than you ever will."

I snarl at him, raising my fist.

"Hit me again, boy, and it'll be the last thing you do."

"Stop it!" Indi screams.

Once again we don't listen.

Anger is filling my veins, making me wild. I lunge at him once more, but he's quick, too quick. He rolls to the side, and by the time I reposition myself and turn, he's got a gun pressed to my head. We're both panting, both wild and angry.

"Do it," I roar. "Take me out of your life like you always fuckin' wanted to."

"I never wanted you out of my life," he growls. "But you won't let me fuckin' speak long enough to tell you what went down."

"I don't want to hear your fuckin' lies!"

He presses the gun harder into my head. "You want me to take your head off?"

"What I want," I snarl, "is to see you dead."

"If you wanted me dead, Dimitri, you would have killed me by now."

"Give me that fuckin' gun, and we'll see how this ends."

Hendrix slowly removes the gun and hands it to me, causing my eyes to widen. He steps back, putting his arms out. Indi screams, but he puts a hand up, stopping her. "You want to kill me, Dimitri? Do it. It's clear to me you're never going to listen to what I have to say. You're going to spend the rest of what is a perfectly good life chasing a man because you can't get over your shit."

Rage swarms through me, causing my head to pound. I lift the gun, blocking out Indi's screams. My hand begins to tremble and sweat trickles down my forehead. This is what I've always wanted. I've always wanted to take his life. To make him pay for what he did. His eyes hold mine, his face expressionless.

I swallow, feeling like sirens are going off in my head.

"Well?" he rasps. "Isn't this what you've always wanted? Or did you want to make me pay first?"

"Please," Indi sobs. "Don't."

I don't look at her; I keep my eyes on him.

"Well, go on!" he roars so loudly it causes me to jerk. "You want to fuckin' kill me then do it. Do it! You're so sure you're right; you're so sure I fucked up your life. If you want to make me pay, here's your chance. Take it now, boy, because if you walk away from here, you'll never get it again."

My vision blurs as emotion rips through my body. Just shoot him. End this. Be free.

"Don't tell me you've come all this way to back down now?"

Thump. Thump. Thump.

It's all I can feel as my vision continues to blur.

"Well?" he roars.

"Shut up!" I snarl, closing my eyes and trying to rein in my emotions.

"I know Jess told you what went down," he says, his voice like ice. "But I'm goin' to repeat it. If you're goin' to shoot me, at least let me tell you what happened. Your momma was in bad shit. I became a pirate to try to fix that—I could do a lot out here that I couldn't do on land. Illegal stuff. It didn't work. When you got beaten because of her behavior, yes, I made her pay by getting her taken out. Her own son copped the punishment for her mistake. That wasn't okay with me. When I came to the hospital, you hated me, despised me. It wasn't fair that I was making it worse . . . so I left. It wasn't until years later that I realized that was the worst thing I could ever have done. Your momma let you down, but what I did was so much worse."

I flinch, struggling to breathe. I have no words, nothing. All the years I wanted to tell him how he fucked my life, but right now all I can do is shake, the gun trembling in my hands.

"I don't expect forgiveness from you, Dimitri. I don't expect you to understand or even try to. But if you're goin' to kill me, you need the fuckin' truth. That's the only thing I can give you that's real. You're my son, even if you don't believe it anymore. And if I'm to die, I want to die with you knowin' that I love you. Always have and always fuckin' will."

His words cause me to sway on my feet. They repeat over and over as the gun slips from my hand. He loves me. He loves me.

"Did you hear me, boy?" he says, his voice less harsh. "I said I love you."

I look up at him and see that he means it, it's written all over his face. It's in that moment I know I can't do it; I can't take his life. There is more than one reason for that. The first being that now I've experienced emotion and loss with a woman, I know I can't take that from Indi. The second is that I believe him. No matter the rage or hatred, I believe what he is saying is true.

In a raspy voice, I croak, "Why didn't you come for me earlier? Why didn't you fuckin' *try?*"

He shakes his head, his eyes on mine. "Because I was an idiot. Because I fucked up. I can't give you any more than that."

I shake my head, trying to clear my vision.

"She loves you," I whisper, my voice too shaky to use. "I don't know why but she does, and . . . I care about her. I can't do it, I can't shoot you and risk the only good thing that's come into my life in a long, long time."

"You know . . ." he says. "She cares about you, too."

I look up. "Then we need to find her."

"I'm tryin'," he says sincerely. "I really am."

I gather myself and look up at him, "Someone took her, and there's only one person who will know who that person was."

Hendrix narrows his eyes. "Who?"

"Livvie."

~

Jess

I wipe my face with a yellow colored washer and try to calm my panting. I've been fighting with Damon for three hours and I'm exhausted. He's determined, though, and has pushed me even when I thought my body couldn't go anymore. Now we're standing having a rest and a drink. I haven't taken my eyes off the guards, who have been watching us, making sure our conversations aren't private.

I don't know how I'm supposed to let him know about Dimitri if they won't stop looking at me.

Suddenly, as if reading my mind, Damon spins around "accidentally" knocking his water all over me. I squeal and grip my shirt, fanning it, frantically trying to keep the freezing water off my skin. I take a step back and my shoe slips on the floor. Damon takes my arm as I go down and his mouth quickly goes past my ear. "A name."

"Dimitri," I say as he pulls me back upright.

His eyes flash and he stares at me for the longest moment. "Dimitri? As in undefeated fighter Dimitri?"

"Hey, get back to work," one of the guarding men yells.

Damon steps back and lets me go, his eyes wide. I nod, letting him know that yes, that is the Dimitri I want. He narrows his gaze but gives me a nod to let me know he understands.

"I think we're done here for the day," he says, wiping his hands on a towel. "I'll see you again tomorrow."

I smile weakly. "Thank you."

He smiles back. "Fight until you can't breathe."

I watch him turn and walk out, and I pray that he can get hold of Dimitri before I have to go back in the cage.

CHAPTER TWENTY-NINE

Jess

Rice, protein and vegetables," Roger grunts, thrusting a tray of food at me. "Eat it all, you need to be strong."

I glare at him, wanting so desperately to beat him. He has no idea of the hatred that swells in my belly every time I look at him. He returns my glare and leans down close.

"You're so lucky I need you for money, otherwise you'd be on your back being fucked like the whore you are."

My fists clench and I grind my jaw, but say nothing.

"You led me on all those years ago, you know that, don't you? Coming in wearing only a towel."

"I was a little girl!" I scream. "It shouldn't have mattered, you shouldn't have looked."

"You used to climb onto my lap," he roars. "You asked for it."

"You're an asshole, a fucking piece of shit. I'll make you pay, I promise you."

"You already made me pay," he snarls, sending spittle over my face. "You fucked my face for life. No one will look at me now. No woman will fuck me. You should be giving it to me, considering you took it."

He reaches down and takes my leg, curling his fingers around my thigh.

"You know," he murmurs. "Fucking you won't affect your fighting."

My entire world stops spinning and I begin to struggle, shoving at him. He grins, as if my struggling completely turns him on. He leans down and grips both of my thighs, pulling them apart. I can't punch him, because my wrists are cuffed. I shake my head from side to side and kick my legs as hard as I can. I only manage to make contact with his thigh. He rears his hand back and slaps me so hard my face jerks to the side.

"You monster, let me go!" I scream, thrashing as best I can.

He presses his hands on the insides of my legs and my vision begins to blur as fear courses through my veins. He slides them up until he reaches my button and then he proceeds to tug my pants down. At least he tries to—I am squirming so much it's next to impossible, but he's managing. Tears tumble down my cheeks as I thrash, trying desperately to figure out a way to escape this. When one of his hands cups my breasts, I begin to dry retch.

"You always fucking loved it," he murmurs. "Loved when I was inside you."

I begin to cry harder, still squirming, still desperately trying to escape. His fingers slide inside my pants and my vision begins to go black. Inside my already damaged mind, I begin to pray.

"Roger!"

I hear Damon's voice pounding on the door and hope swells in my chest. Roger snarls and pulls his hand from my pants, getting to his feet. He swings the door open and barks, "What?"

"There's an urgent visitor. I'll watch her."

Roger turns and grins at me. "Enjoy your dinner."

He leaves and I crumble. I begin sobbing so hard my body shakes. Damon steps in and closes the door before walking over and kneeling in front of me. He takes one look at my unbuttoned pants and the way I'm shaking, and a curse leaves his mouth. He reaches out and touches my cheek gently. "All the teaching I gave and not once did I think about how to teach you to fight off a predator. How long has he been . . . ?"

"I . . ." My voice trembles. "He did it first when I was twelve. It continued. When I was sixteen I got away and haven't seen him again until recently."

"How'd you get away?" he asks, his voice tight.

"I stabbed him . . . a lot."

His eyes widen. "*You* did that to his face?"

I nod, feeling my lip tremble. "I thought he was dead and . . . then he showed up at one of Dimitri's fights."

"Is Dimitri your . . . lover?"

I nod again, dropping my head. "I don't even know if he will guess where I am. If he doesn't find me, Roger will . . . will . . ."

"Hey," Damon says, lifting my chin and meeting my gaze. "He won't touch you, I'll find a way to make sure of that. I'll get to Dimitri."

"Why can't you get me out of here?" I whisper.

He drops his head. "Because Roger gives me good money for what I do. Without that money I can't support my family. My wife was in an accident four years ago. She's completely disabled now and it's around the clock care. That kind of care isn't cheap and so I'm working to train illegal fighters to make enough money to keep us afloat. If he suspects . . ."

"I understand," I whisper, cutting him off.

He looks me dead in the eye. "But I will get you out of here, I'll find Dimitri."

"When you do, tell him . . . tell him L-L-Livvie knows where I am."

He nods and stands. "If I stay too long, he will get suspicious. Eat, you need your strength. I'll stand guard tonight, don't worry about Rex . . . ahh . . . Roger. I'll make sure he doesn't come in, I'll figure a good excuse out. You'll be safe to sleep."

I smile weakly. "Thank you, I can't tell you how much this means to me."

He smiles back. "I think I can guess."

He turns and leaves the room and I slump in relief. I hope to God he can find a way to get me out of here, because if he can't there'll only be so long I can fight Roger off. Eventually, he'll find out a way to get to me and if he does, he'll take everything I've fought so hard to build up. I drop my head and tug on my cuffs. How the fuck am I supposed to eat when I'm shackled?

With a sigh, I reach both hands out and bring the tray closer to me. It's got some plain rice, vegetables and some sort of stew-like concoction. I use the fork in both hands and I stab it into a piece of broccoli. I carefully bring up both hands and place it in my mouth—okay, so that wasn't as hard as I first thought. I do this over and over until I've got most of my plate finished. I have dropped a few pieces on my pants but I manage to clear them off with great difficulty.

When I'm done, I lie down and curl onto my side. My ribs are aching and my heart is sore. I want to go home, to the only people I care about. I don't want to be here, not knowing what each day will hold. I could go into the fight and end up getting killed before Dimitri reaches me, or I could do well and only encourage Roger more. I close my eyes and take a deep, steadying breath.

Above all else, I have to stay strong.

Strength is the only thing I have left.

~

"Move," Roger growls, shoving me through the massive crowd.

My knees begin to tremble as I stare at the hundreds of people surrounding the large cage in the middle of the old warehouse we're in. It's the night of my first fight and I'm not feeling confident at all. Damon spent another day with me, but while I think I know enough, I'm still not sure that I'll make it out of here unscathed.

"In there," Damon says from behind me.

He told me he's trying to find Dimitri, but he's hoping to get some straight answers here tonight. He's also going to have my back in the cage. In other words, he'll be the one yelling at me to keep me focused. We step out into a back room that looks very familiar to the ones I've been in when Dimi has fought. Roger storms over to a locker and slams his fist down over it, swinging it open.

He pulls out a set of small cotton shorts and a crop top. He walks over and shoves them at me. I stare down at them. That's it? He wants me to fight wearing next to nothing? There's nothing here that will protect my body at all.

"Stop staring and get ready, we start in ten."

I give Damon a look and he nods at me. I go to step away to get changed, only to have Roger take my arm and squeeze it. "You get changed here."

"There are people around," I protest.

He leans in closer. "You want me to take you out back and change you myself?"

My skin crawls.

"No? I didn't think so. Then you change here."

Hesitating, I slowly pull my top off, thankful for the invention of bras. I pull on the tiny crop top and then manage to unclip and remove my bra without showing any breast. Then I drop my pants and slip into the cotton shorts. Roger spins me around, a seedy expression on his face. He grins at me and I fight the urge to spit in his face. He takes hold of my hands and jerks them out in front of him, strapping them. When he's done, he stands back and looks over at Damon.

"I hope she's ready."

"She's as ready as she can be after two days," Damon snaps.

"Remember, fight or get fucked up," Roger says to me. "No one will be saving you if she beats the shit out of you; you're all you have in there. Make it count."

I take a deep breath and try to remember everything Damon has taught me. I can't let him down right now. I turn when Roger does and follow him out into the large crowd again. People stare, taunt, cheer, poke and shove me as we pass through. They're wild, off their trees on drugs and alcohol. Some of them are waving around hundreds of dollars' worth of cash.

"Here we are again," a voice comes booming across the loudspeaker. "Who's ready to fiiiight?"

The crowd goes wild and I cover my ears, cringing. They're all sick, watching women fight like this. Roger shoves me up onto the small stage beside the cage and I catch my first glimpse of my opponent. She's bigger than me without a doubt, but Damon has taught me to fight someone bigger so I am slightly relieved. The bad thing, however, is that not only is she bigger than me but she's also a great deal . . . chunkier. She's got quite a decent amount of fat on her body, which could be a problem for doing damage.

"We've got two new contestants for you tonight!" the man roars into his microphone. "Rex Rock's new girl, Blair, and Jay Jarrod's new girl, Pinkie. Who's ready to see them fight?"

Rex Rock? Seriously?

The crowd screams and I find myself being shoved into the cage. When we're in, the door's slammed closed. I suddenly feel claustrophobic, wanting to get out. I turn with shaky knees and face my opponent. She's glaring at me, lips pursed, legs spread and ready. I get myself into the best stance I can and try to block out the rest of the world.

Fight until your last breath.

"One!"

I lift my fists, staring her right in the eye.

"Two!"

She wipes a drop of sweat off her forehead and grins at me.

"Three!"

She charges first, just like Damon said. She also swings high. Feeling my chest swell with hope, I duck her fist and drive mine into her stomach only to find she barely flinches. Fear courses through my veins as she reaches down, gripping my hair and pulling me backwards so hard I feel some of it being pulled free. When my head is back she drives a fist into my mouth, splitting my lip wide open.

"Blair!" I hear Damon roar. "Remember what I taught you. Focus."

The girl hits me again, still holding my hair tightly.

"She's a fucking failure!" Roger bellows. "You can kiss your job goodbye, Damon."

No. Damon. I snap my eyes open and, after a second, take in the position I'm in. She's got my hair, yes, but she's left my arms and legs wide open. With all my might, I swing my leg back and I bring it right up into her groin. A scream escapes her throat as her fingers uncurl from my hair and she stumbles backwards. Like Damon said, her body automatically doubles over and so I charge forward, taking hold of her hair and bringing my knee up into her face.

I feel her nose bust open against my leg, and I have to fight back the good in me and remember that the only way for me to get out of here is to fight and not think. Her hand flies up to her nose and she straightens, swinging her fist aimlessly. I duck it and instead ram another fist into her groin, bringing her down to her knees. I take the chance to launch at her, using my foot to hit her so hard in the face she goes flat on her back. The crowd is roaring so loudly I can't hear myself think.

"One!"

She doesn't move; she's choking on her own blood.

"Two!"

Should I help her? God. I'm a monster.

"Three!"

The noise from the crowd has me momentarily deafened. Before I know what's happening, Damon is in the cage and taking hold of my face, saying something I can't understand through the noise. Roger comes barreling in and the victorious smile on his face tells me I've won this fight.

"And it looks like this fight is owned by Blair!" the emcee yells.

The crowd roars again as Damon leads me off the stage and out back.

"You won!" he says as soon as the door is closed behind us.

I stare at him, still completely in shock. I won? I won?

"I won," I whisper.

He leans in close, taking my face in his hands. "You live to survive another day, and another day means you're a step closer to getting out of here."

I smile now.

He's right—the longer I last, the longer Dimitri has to find me.

Maybe there's hope after all.

CHAPTER THIRTY

Dimitri

My phone rings, stirring me from my sleep. I'd only just drifted off after days of trying to track down Livvie, who disappeared when we were still on land. I've worked for at least twenty-four hours straight, but I had no leads and felt myself dropping off to sleep at Hendrix's desk. Now my phone is ringing. I lift my head and stare at the screen. I don't recognize the number but I'm not missing one call until I've found Jess.

"Yeah?" I mutter, answering it.

"Is this Dimitri?"

I don't recognize the male voice.

"Yeah, who's this?"

He's silent a minute.

"Hello?"

"Sorry, my name is Damon. You're a hard man to track down."

"Do I know you?"

"No," he says. "But I have information for you."

"What about?"

"Blair."

Blair . . . My eyes suddenly pop open.

"Is this a fuckin' trick."

"No, it's not. My name is Damon and I work for Roger. I teach his fighters how to fight. He has Blair."

Roger. Roger has her? My head spins and wild anger swells in my chest as I imagine all the fucked up things he's doing to her.

"Tell me she's okay?" I rasp.

He sighs. "He's got her fighting, Dimitri. So I guess in the scheme of things, for now she's okay. Though she's had the fucking shit beaten out of her by two opponents so far. He put her in her first real fight last night. She won."

That's my girl, that's my fucking amazing girl. Fighting to survive.

"How badly is she hurt?"

"A few cracked ribs, split lips, a couple of black eyes."

"Fuck," I growl, clenching my fists.

"It could be worse," he mutters. "I've already stopped him from—"

"From what?" I bark.

"From raping her, Dimitri. I can't promise that I'll be able to stop it for long. You need to get to her."

"Where is she?"

He gives me a location and I curse loudly. "I'm at least two days away."

"You'd better hurry the fuck up, because he's jumping the queue with the fights. He's putting her in another one in two nights, but, Dimitri, she's going up against Fire Cat."

My body stiffens. Fire Cat is one of the best women fighters there is underground. Jess, no matter how strong, would never be able to fight her.

"She'll crumble."

"You're tellin' me," he says. "I'm doing my best to train her in time, but you need to get here before then. If she goes in that cage, she'll be killed."

"I'm going to be there, you tell her . . . I'll be there."

"Hurry."

He clicks the phone off and I drop mine, turning and charging out of the room. I make it into the dining room where Hendrix and the boys are still partying. At my entrance, Hendrix stands.

"What is it?"

"I know where she is."

His eyes widen and Indi stands up beside him, her expression full of fear. "Where?" she asks.

"Roger has her."

"Fuck!" Hendrix barks.

"It gets worse—he's got her fighting. Her next fight is in two days and she's going up against one of the best female fighters there is. We can't let her get in that cage."

"How long until we can get there?" Hendrix asks.

"I don't know that we'll do it in two days," I say, feeling that familiar tightening in my chest again.

"We'll fuckin' get there," Hendrix growls. "Men! Let's move. We need to push this baby up to full speed."

I give Hendrix the address and walk up onto the deck, gripping the railings so hard my knuckles ache. If I don't make it in time— if she dies or is severely injured because of me—I'll never forgive myself. I let her down, I believed she had run instead of even thinking she might have been taken. If it wasn't for my fuckin' mistake, I could have found her earlier.

"Are you okay?"

I turn to see Indi staring at me, her face full of concern.

"How can I be fuckin' okay? I thought she'd come back to Hendrix. If I didn't have my head rammed so far up my ass, I would have gotten to her sooner."

"It's not your fault, Dimitri."

I spin around. "Then whose fault is it?"

She tilts her head and studies me. "You love her, don't you?"

I turn away, clenching my fists.

"It's okay to feel like that," she says softly. "You should never fight how you feel."

"She changed me. She made me see things differently. No matter what I did, she always had a way of coming back at me and completely throwing me. She never showed fear. But she'll be scared now, Indigo. She'll be so fucking scared."

"She's a tough girl, she'll fight for those she loves."

I shake my head. "You don't understand . . . if she gets in that cage, she won't be coming back out. He's putting her in a death trap."

"That fighter, she won't kill her . . . will she?"

I turn and stare into her eyes. "She's killed before and with someone Jess's size, she'll do it again."

She makes a small squeaking sound. I know I shouldn't be so blunt with her but she has to know. She can't live in fantasy. Her friend is in danger and if we don't get to her in time, she'll likely be killed or beaten so severely her face won't ever be the same again.

"We have to get to her, and we have to be quick about it."

Indi nods.

She knows I'm right.

CHAPTER THIRTY-ONE

Jess

He's coming for you," Damon whispers as he spins me around, pressing me to his back. "Now get out of my grip."

"He's coming?" I ask, feeling something big and emotional swelling in my chest.

"He's coming, but I can't promise it'll be before this fight."

My heart sinks.

"She's going to fuck me up, isn't she?"

He grumbles and holds me tighter. "It's not looking good. Now get out of my grip."

I take hold of one of his fingers and twist it so far back he groans. "Nice try, but if I was using strength . . ." He pulls his finger back down, showing me I'd never be strong enough to pull it if he was trying. "You need to do better than that."

"Where is he?" I ask, lifting my foot and stomping hard on one of his.

"Ow, shit. That's a great move except your opponent probably has shoes. He's out at sea."

Out at sea? Why the fuck is he out at sea?

"Why is he not on land?" I growl, lifting my leg and shoving it backwards into his shin.

"Good, that's a good move," he groans, hopping slightly. "And he's out there looking for you."

Looking for me? Why would he think I'm on the ocean? Oh God, he thinks Hendrix has me. He's taken himself out on the ocean and so far away from where I really am.

"He's coming back as quickly as he can. Don't doubt that."

"But there's a huge chance it won't be quick enough, right?"

"Right," he says, putting me in a headlock.

"Ow, you're hurting me, you great big bully," I mutter, squirming.

"Suck it up. She's going to hurt you a whole lot more if you don't start paying attention. Get Dimitri off your mind and focus on this. He's not here right now and the chances are high that you're going to be in this fight. You need to put everything you can into it."

"Fine," I grumble. "But know this . . . I'm not happy about going up against Catwoman."

He chuckles. "Fire Cat?"

"What sort of name is Fire Cat anyway?" I mutter, reaching up and pinching his skin so hard I draw blood. His arm flies away from my neck.

"Jesus, that fuckin' hurt."

I grin at him. "You didn't teach me that one, did you?"

He grins back at me. "Apparently running with pirates has done you some good."

"If you gave me a gun, I'd knock Cat's fire right out of her."

He chuckles. "I don't doubt it."

He gets into the fighter stance and I do too. He begins swinging soft punches and I begin ducking them.

"So, why Fire Cat?" I ask, panting and ducking between his flying fists.

"You'll see when you're face to face with her. You think your hair is red . . ."

"Okay," I grunt as he pops me in the belly. So that explains the fire part, but what about the cat part?"

He snorts. "She's got these . . . claws."

I stop and he swings, hitting me softly in the cheek. He gives me a *whoopsie* look.

"Explain claws?"

He looks hesitant.

"Now, Damon."

"She's got enhanced claws."

I don't feel so well.

"Enhanced?"

"She's had some freaky fucking operation. You know how some people can actually get fake horns in their skulls?"

"Yessss . . ."

"Well . . . she got fake claws."

"You're joking, right?" I say, feeling my stomach turn.

"No, I'm not joking. The woman is crazy, like a cat on roids."

"Roids?"

"Steroids."

"Great. What chance have I got up against a mental cat woman with fake claws?" I cry, dropping down into a squat and cupping my head in my hands.

"You've got a chance. She's a big girl, Blair, and she's slow. You're super quick. If you're careful, you can have her down in a timely manner."

"Seriously?" I bark, looking up at him. "You're such a liar."

He frowns. "I'm not lying."

"I can't have her down in a timely fucking manner, she's got fake claws, for Christ's sakes."

He chews on his lower lip. "Okay, so maybe it won't be timely."

"She'll gouge my eyes out."

He looks ill.

"Then she'll probably poke holes in my face."

He scrunches up his lips.

"She'll—"

"Okay," he says, throwing his hands up. "I'll do the best I can to help you, but I can't promise you're not going to have to go into that ring with her."

I swallow and turn away, unable to shake the sick feeling in my stomach.

"Then teach me how to avoid her hands, at least get a few solid shots in."

"That I can do," he says. "Let's get to it."

I sigh and turn back to him.

Even with him teaching me, I just don't know if it'll be enough.

~

The sound the crowd is making is deafening. There are triple the people at this fight than my last. Damon has been training me for two solid days, teaching me the best moves he can to keep me clear of Fire Cat's claws. It doesn't take away the nauseating feeling in my stomach at the thought that I'm going up against someone who has a goddamned weapon. It shouldn't be allowed, but this is illegal fighting after all.

Roger is beside me, snarling rules into my ear that I can't hear. All I want to do is beat him and throw him in the ring with the crazy cat lady, but I can't. I can only pray that Dimitri shows up. I've been searching the crowd for him, or Hendrix, or someone, but so far there's nothing—no familiar faces, no hope for me to hold on to.

"Are you listening to me?" Roger barks.

"I'm fucking listening," I snarl, shoving through the people.

"You need to be paying attention. If you look away for even a second she'll have you."

"I heard you!"

He takes me into the back room where the long process of getting prepared starts. I'm dressed, my hands are bound and my hair is pulled back. Damon comes in looking worried just before I'm about to go out.

"What is it?" I ask.

"Nothing," he murmurs, staring at nothing.

"Damon . . ."

He turns back to me. "It's fine. You'll be fine."

He doesn't look convinced and suddenly I feel sick. Roger takes my arm just as I hear the sounds of the man on the microphone introducing the fight. My legs seem to halt as realization kicks in. He's going to make me fight. Dimitri isn't here. This girl could damage my face permanently.

"I can't," I cry, struggling.

Roger turns around and he slaps me hard across the face.

"You can and you fucking will. You don't get a choice."

"Rex!" Damon barks. "You want her to win?"

"You know I fucking do," Roger snarls.

"Then you fuckin' keep your hands off."

They have a glaring contest before Roger turns to me. Then he reaches into his pants and pulls out a gun. He's got the cold metal pressed to my head before I can even flinch.

"You have two choices. Fight or die. You want to fuckin' die, I'll kill you right here."

"Put that down," Damon snarls.

Roger ignores him.

My entire world begins to spin at the feeling of having a gun to my head. I begin to shake and sweat trickles down my cheek.

"F-f-f-f-fight," I whisper.

"What's that?" he yells, pressing the gun into my flesh harder.

"Fight!" I scream.

He grins and puts the gun back into his pocket.

"That's what I thought."

CHAPTER THIRTY-TWO

Jess

I stare at Fire Cat as we wait in the ring for the final countdown. My heart is thudding and I can't help but stare at her hands. Damon was right, she's got these claws coming out of her fingertips. They're two inches long at least and they look lethal; I don't know how she manages to do anything with them on. She's a bigger girl, Damon was right about that too, and she's got fiery red hair.

She's quite butch.

"Are you all ready to rummmmmmble!" the emcee asks and the crowd screams.

I blink rapidly, repeating all Damon's words in my head. Focus, Jess. You can do this, just keep your eyes on her hands at all times. Focus on going for the parts she leaves open. You can do this. You can win this. You just have to get through this and Dimitri will be here—he'll save you and things will be okay.

"One!"

My world spins and I can hear nothing but the sound of my own heart.

"Two!"

I can't do it, I can't fucking do it. She'll kill me. I want to go home. My eyes burn.

"Jess, head up and fight," Damon yells.

I lift my head, staring her right in the eyes. You have to do this—you have to.

"Three."

I lunge before she does and I slide right to the floor. Her hand swings but it swings in the air, and I know it's because she expected me to go high. Instead I did a baseball style slide right to her feet. When I get to her feet, I jerk my fist back and I punch her hard in the kneecap. She stumbles backwards slashing at my head. I roll to the side quickly, getting a vision of her before jumping to my feet.

She spins around, her eyes wild as she lunges toward me. Her hands fly out and her claws come right to my face. At the last moment I duck and drive my head into her stomach. She makes a choking sound and her claws come down, clawing at the bare skin on my back. I scream in agony as they scratch against my skin. I can't feel any blood and I'm almost sure she didn't break my skin, but if that's how much it hurts to get "grazed" then I don't want to know what the real thing feels like.

"Some amazing fighter," I taunt her as I quickly roll and slide away from her. "You're not a good fighter. If you were you wouldn't be wearing those things."

She scowls at me and lifts her foot, twisting quickly and so fast I barely see her. I feel her, though, when her foot connects with the side of my head. I spin to the left, crying out in pain as my vision swims for a moment. I can't stay here—if I don't move she'll—Another kick, right to my back. I stumble forward, gasping for air as all the wind is knocked out of me.

"Twist, Blair!" Damon roars.

I twist my body just as a foot comes soaring through the air at me. She misses me but only by a second. It's enough. While she catches her balance, I lift my own foot and I kick her so hard at the backs of her knees, she loses her footing and falls. She hits the ground with a thump and one of her own fingernails pierces her arm, sending a shrill screech across the crowd.

It goes wild.

I launch myself into the air and I land so hard on her back I feel something crack. She's quick, though, and good. I made a mistake jumping on her. She tangles her legs in mine and with a strength I've never witnessed from a woman, she flips me over using her body until I land on my back. She raises her elbow and I scream as it comes barreling down toward my face, crashing against my cheek.

"Jess!"

I hear a sound, a familiar sound, but I don't know where it's coming from. I can't focus on it, I have to think. When she raises her elbow again, I turn my head to the side and I bite down on her arm so hard I draw blood. She squeals loudly and stumbles off me, gripping her arm the best she can without doing more damage. I lunge at her, exhausted and sore, but needing to keep fighting.

I wrap my arm around her from behind and I jerk her backwards. She lifts her claw and stabs it into my hand. The pain is excruciating and I can't hold on. I fall away, clutching my hand as blood pours out of a deep, ugly wound.

"Jess!"

Dimitri?

I spin around and stare into the crowd and there he is, standing at the side of the cage, staring in at me with fear in his eyes.

"Dimi," I mouth.

"Watch out!"

I feel something smash me hard across the back of my head before everything goes black.

CHAPTER THIRTY-THREE

Jess

Y ou fucking useless piece of shit!"
I hear someone roaring at me, and I blink my eyes open to see
Roger storming toward me. I'm in the back room and I've clearly been
tossed on the ground. My body aches, my head throbs and my hand is
covered in dried blood. Before I can focus too heavily on my situation,
Roger has hold of my shirt and is launching me into the air.

"You lost me a fuck load of money and for that you'll pay."

He shoves me back down, hard. I cry out and grip my head,
trying to stop the pounding. I stare in horror as Roger pulls out a
gun and aims it at me.

"You should have died a long time ago, Blair. I should have
fucked you until you were nothing but a broken shell and then I
should have killed you slowly."

He grins at me. Oh God, he's going to do it. He's going to kill
me and he'll probably get away with it.

"You did kill me," I cry, trying to distract him. Dimitri was
out there. He was. I saw him. Where is he now? "You did break my
body until it was no more than a shell."

"And yet you're still living, still fucking around like the whore
you are."

I feel my entire body begin to trembling with a fear I've never felt before in my life.

"You think I don't know you've let Dimitri put his dick inside you."

My face pales.

"You didn't think he was going to save you, did you? Aw, poor sweet Blair. You're forgetting something," he murmurs, cocking the gun. "No one cares about you."

"You're wrong about that."

I hear the sound of Dimitri's voice and then the booming sound of a gunshot. I close my eyes, pressing my hands over my ears, too scared to open them. If Roger got the first shot in . . . oh God.

"I care about her," I hear softly.

I dare to open my eyes, and when I do I see Dimitri at the door, followed by Luke, Hendrix and Drake. My heart both breaks to pieces and mends back together all at the same time. I let out a choking sob as Dimitri kneels in front of me, scooping me into his arms.

"I got you, baby. Ain't nobody goin' to hurt you again."

I glance at the ground as he moves to the side and I see Roger's dead body, blood seeping from a tiny hole in his head.

"He's d-d-d-dead?" I rasp.

"He's dead. Never goin' to hurt you again."

I press my face into Dimitri's shirt and I breathe him in. He smells exactly like everything I've needed so desperately in the past week. He smells like home. Like comfort. Like family.

"Hendrix, you and your boys able to clean this up?" Dimitri asks.

"On it."

I lift my head, staring at the two of them. They're in the same room, both alive, both speaking . . . civilly.

"You two . . . you're . . ." I croak.

"We're fine," Hendrix says, walking over and grinning down at me. "You fought real good out there tonight, made me real proud."

I try to smile but I can't. Tears decide to break free instead. He strokes my cheek and looks up at Dimitri. "Get her someplace and clean her up. We've got this here."

"Damon," I say as Dimitri takes me from the room. "Where is he?"

Dimitri looks down at me, his blue eyes full of things I don't quite understand. One of them I'm sure is relief. The rest is a mystery. "He's in the crowd, making sure no one comes in here."

"He's a good man. He has a family, a wife that's . . . well . . . disabled. He needs the money this job brings."

Dimitri smiles at me. "I paid him very accordingly for taking care of you."

"You did?" I squeak.

He strokes my cheek. "Yeah, baby, I did."

I let myself relax back into his arms.

"Take her home, we've got this covered," Drake says, smiling down at me.

I haven't seen him for a while now, but I adore Drake.

"Hey, Drake."

"Hey, good to see you're still alive."

I smile as Dimitri carries me through the back entrance and out into the street. When we reach his car, he opens the door and puts me in.

"Dimi?" I ask as he climbs in the driver's seat.

He looks over at me, reaching across and taking my face in his hands. He runs his thumbs over my swelling cheekbones.

"I'm so fuckin' sorry, Jess," he rasps.

"You don't need to be sorry, it wasn't your fault."

He smoothes a finger over my bottom lip. "You have no idea how I felt when I found out you were fightin'. Shit, Jess, I thought I'd be too late . . ."

I reach up and cup his jaw. "You're not, though."

He leans in, pressing a soft kiss to the side of my mouth. "You made me real proud out there tonight, Hendrix was right about that. You fought so fuckin' well."

I nestle my head into his shoulder and breathe him in. "I was scared, Dimi."

"I know, baby," he murmurs into my hair.

"Take me home."

"I'm on it."

He leans back and starts the car. I clip myself in.

"Are you going to get into trouble for killing Roger?" I whisper, shuddering at the thought that Roger could bring the person I love harm even after he's dead.

"No, because Roger is a criminal and he runs illegal clubs. He's not going to be missed and he's certainly not going to have anyone looking for him. Those who do look for him won't look very long before realizing he's gone and moving on. You're safe now, Jess. I won't let anyone hurt you again, do you understand me?"

I turn and stare into his eyes. "I understand."

"I didn't say it to you before, and I should have, because God knows you deserve it more than anyone. You need to know . . ." He hesitates. "You need to know I want you in my life, for as long as you'll have me."

I force my lips not to tremble at his words; instead I let a tear slip down my cheek. He stares at it, a muscle in his jaw ticking. Then he turns his eyes to the road and begins to drive. In the darkness reality finally hits. I realize just how close I came to having my life upended for a final time. My body begins to tremble and tears start flowing hard and fast while I make soft, squeaking sounds.

"Shit," Dimitri says.

The car swerves to the side of the road and Dimitri's door swings open. He's at mine in less than a minute, swinging the door open and pulling me into his arms. I crumble into him, sobbing so heavily I'm unable to make a single sound; my body is just shaking violently.

"Baby, you're okay," Dimitri soothes, pulling me out of the car and switching us so he's sitting down and I'm tucked into his lap.

He holds me there for what feels like hours, stroking my hair and soothing me. I feel my body beginning to go numb from lack of movement, and I have no doubt he's feeling exactly the same. He doesn't say anything, he doesn't have to. He's being everything he needs to be in this moment—he's comforting me, he's letting me know he's here with me and that it's all going to be okay now.

That's all I need to know.

~

Dimitri

"She's okay," I say, letting Hendrix and Indi in.

Hendrix shifts his eyes to the bed where Jess is sleeping. I can see the concern there, and for the first time I can see how much he really does care about her. She was right all along—to her he's a hero. He saved her life and he gave her a chance to live again. She's willing to give everything to him and now I can finally see—she has a right to.

"She been sleeping long?" Hendrix asks.

"About two hours. I gave her painkillers and she passed out."

"The damage?"

I feel my chest tighten with rage at what that son of a bitch did to her.

"She's got bruised ribs, a few bits of damage on her face but thankfully, there's nothing major. She'll feel better in a few days.

She's a tough girl, and she's very lucky that things didn't end far worse for her. I was worried she had a concussion but she seems to be fine."

"Should we take her to a doctor?" Indi asks.

I shake my head. "Unless we see something change dramatically, then no."

She nods, gripping Hendrix's hand so tight her fingers are white.

"She's all right," I say, and she meets my gaze.

"But what about . . . ? What about her mind."

It's Hendrix who answers that for me.

"She's got a stronger mind than most, she'll get through it."

I nod, staring at her. She's curled on her side and her red hair is fanned out over the pillow. After I managed to get her showered and changed, she just collapsed onto the bed. I tried to get her to eat but she wasn't interested. I figure right now, more than anything, she needs to just come down from the events she's lived through.

"We're in the next room," Hendrix says. "If you need anything just yell out."

I nod again.

"Son?" he says and my body stiffens at the word.

I turn slowly to him, feeling my jaw tightening.

"Thank you," he says, holding my gaze before turning and leaving.

I let the breath out I didn't realize I was holding. I lock the door once they're gone and I remove my shirt quickly, before climbing into bed beside Jess. She turns, tucking herself into my body. I wrap my arms around her and breathe her in.

Thankful that I've been given such an amazing gift.

I won't let that gift go.

CHAPTER THIRTY-FOUR

Jess

Please," I whisper, sliding my tongue down his abs.

"Fuck, baby," he groans, arching his hips up. "You need to stop."

"I don't want to stop."

"You're still sore."

I nip the flesh just above the hard ridge of his cock. He makes a strangled groaning sound and flexes his hips. I slowly slide down lower, until his cock brushes against my cheek. I turn my face into it, letting the tip run along my lips. God, I so desperately want to taste him. Sore or not. I need him. I need all of him. I part my lips and slip him inside, relishing in the feeling of him filling and stretching my mouth.

"Fuck, oh fuck," he rasps above me, bringing his hands down to rest on my head.

I slowly snake my tongue out and slide it around his aching shaft. He growls deep and low and his fingers tangle in my hair. I begin to slide my lips up and down, feeling the way his cock swells beneath them. Tingles break out over my skin and my pussy clenches with raw need. I want him inside me, but more, I want to feel him release all around me. I want to watch him come undone.

"Suck me, baby," he groans. "Suck me so fuckin' hard."

I tremble and I suck him hard, as hard as he needs. I pick up the pace, using my hand to stroke the base while I rotate my lips over his head, sucking and nipping, pulling and jerking, until he's arching his back and bellowing my name.

"Going to come, fuck, pull . . . out . . ."

I don't.

I suck harder, I suck faster. My free hand finds his balls and I cup them, giving him a little squeeze until he's shooting his release into the back of my throat. I take all of him, sucking until he begins to grow soft and his cries of pleasure have died down. Then I slip him out of my mouth and I slowly slide up his body, taking in every inch of hard flesh that makes contact with my body as I move. When I get up to his face, he wraps his arms around me and stares at me with lust-filled eyes.

"You suck cock like a pro," he murmurs, staring at my swollen lips.

I giggle softly. "It's my specialty."

He chuckles and his hands come up to cup my naked breasts.

"What about you?"

"What about me?" I grin.

He grins back, big and devilish.

"I can't leave you hanging, I can't leave that pretty pussy throbbing."

I stare at him with a confused expression. "Oh, honey," I begin in a sultry voice. "You didn't think you were good enough to get my pussy throbbing, did you?"

His eyes widen and his grin gets bigger. Then he flips me until I'm on my back.

"So you're saying my cock did nothing for you?"

I shake my head with a wicked grin. "I'm sorry to offend you, it's just . . . well, you know . . . it wasn't that good."

He leans back and takes my knees, spreading them.

"Funny, from this angle you're glistening."

I shrug, but my cheeks heat with need. "I'm always glistening, it's part of the job."

He tilts his head to the side. "Is that so? So if I put my mouth . . . say . . ." He leans down and presses his lips to my clit. "Here . . . you won't scream my name?"

I jerk and I begin to pant. "No, not at all," I breathe.

"Are you sure about that?" he murmurs, snaking his tongue out and flicking my clit.

"Positive," I gasp.

"Shame," he says, sucking it into his mouth.

I buck my hips. "Oh God."

He stops and pulls back, licking his lips. "Well, considering you don't like it . . . I've had my taste. Are we done here?"

I groan. "I take it back." I thrust my hips. "Suck me."

He grins. "Where, baby? You need to be more specific."

"My clit. God, suck my clit."

With wild eyes, he drops down and devours me. He sucks me deep and hard, his tongue destroying all my strength. His mouth is heaven, his lips are perfect, and I don't ever want it to end.

And when I come, I come so hard I've no doubt the entire hotel has heard my screams.

~

"I've heard it's a great club," Indi says as we walk down the street three nights later.

We've decided before we get back to business that we'll have a few days to chill out. Now that Hendrix and Dimitri aren't trying to kill each other (mostly) we have the chance to spend some time together. The two men are still stiff and struggle to have conversation, but Indi told me about the big breakdown and fight on the ship, and I figure, now the ice has been broken, they can slowly work toward maybe one day having a good relationship.

"Me too," I say, answering Indi.

"How are you feeling?"

I shrug. "Still a little sore, but nothing incredibly major."

"You're lucky," she says, giving me a concerned expression.

I nod. "I know."

"At least it's over now. He's gone and you can finally live the life you never thought you were going to have."

I smile. "You don't know how much that means to me."

"No," she agrees. "I don't think I do. But . . . I think Dimitri does."

I flush. "Me too."

"Do you think he's the one you're going to spend that time with?"

I turn and look at the gorgeous man behind me, who is dressed entirely in black and looks like a bad-ass. His hair is whipping around his face, his blue eyes are bright and, shit, he looks so good I'm tempted to just take him to an alley and make him fuck me until I can't breathe. He winks at me and I feel my pussy clench. Shit.

"Oh yeah," I answer Indi. "I am almost sure it's going to be him."

She smiles and we line up at the club. The moment Dimitri reaches me, his arms go around me and his lips slide up my neck. "That look you just gave me—you're lucky I didn't take you out back and fuck you so hard you screamed my name so loudly the entire club heard you."

I tremble. "I believe I had a similar thought."

He kisses my jaw and his hands slide up to my breasts. "We can still go back."

"You two!" Indi says. "Keep it together."

Hendrix slaps her ass. "You're thinkin' the same thing, darlin', and you're going to get it."

Indi flushes and giggles just as Luke appears with Drake. I smile at both of them. Drake grins at me and Luke nods, but he's got a slight smile on his lips. We shuffle through the crowd and finally make our way into the club. The music is thumping and people are wiggling in tight little groups under the dark blue light. Dimitri takes my hand and pulls me through until he finds us all a booth.

"Drink?" he says into my ear.

I nod with a smile and he disappears with Hendrix. Luke and Drake slide in beside us and I turn to them. "Are you enjoying your break?" I ask Luke.

He nods. "It's been a good break after recent events."

I smile, completely agreeing with him. "It was a hard time for all of us."

He nods again. "You're telling me. That night you went missing I thought Dimitri was going to lose his shit."

I frown. "I feel so bad for worrying him."

Luke laughs. "When Livvie came in and said you had run, I thought he was going to tear her head off. He was so angry. So mad and wild."

I shake my head, confused. I knew Livvie had told Dimitri that I'd run, but I hadn't thought he'd believed her right off the bat. I'd figured he'd searched for me before maybe considering that I'd run.

"How long did he look for me before he actually believed I'd run?"

Luke looks confused.

"Tell me, Luke."

"I'm not tryin' to cause a fight here, Jess."

"Please," I say, and I know my face is tight.

"He didn't look for you," he sighs. "He went straight to the ship and to Hendrix. He thought you'd gone back to him and you can't blame him for that, he—"

"What did he say?" I ask, my voice strained. "When he found out. Was there even a second he doubted Livvie's story? Even a fucking second?"

Luke swallows and looks around nervously. "He was upset, he thought you had run. He wanted to make you pay for using him and he wasn't thinking . . ."

"He wanted to make me . . . *pay*? Did he say that?" I growl.

He puts his head in his hands.

"Luke!"

"Yes," he yells. "But you can't entirely blame him. You were his captive, after all."

"You have no idea," I snarl, standing.

"No, maybe I don't. That's why you need to take this up with him."

"I'll do that right now."

I shove my way out of the booth.

"Jess!" Luke says, standing.

I'm tearing through the crowd before he can stop me. I get to the bar and when I see Dimitri, I take his arm. He turns to me, but before he can even open his mouth I am yelling.

"When you found out I was missing, what did you say?"

He looks confused. "What?"

"You heard me, Dimitri. And don't you fucking lie to me, or I'll walk out. When Livvie came and told you that I was gone, what was your first reaction?"

His jaw tightens. "I was fucking mad, Jess. I thought you'd run. I thought you'd used me and then taken your chance to run—"

"How could you?" I cry. "I understand she made it look real, but you didn't, even for a fucking second, think that she was lying? After everything we shared, you just assumed I would run, just like that?"

He opens his mouth to speak, but I cut him off.

"I didn't run the first time you left me in a hotel. If I was going to go, I would have done it then. Fuck, Dimitri, I gave you my body and I trusted you with something I'd never given anyone else and you instantly believed that dirty slut. You didn't even give me a chance, because if you had, you would have considered that something bad had happened."

He flinches.

"Did you even look for me? Did you even search the crowd, or the streets, or your house, before storming to that ship?"

He doesn't answer but it's the only answer I need. My eyes well with tears. "I got taken, I got forced to fight, I was charged at by a psychotic, red-headed, big, crazy woman who grew herself fucking claws . . . all because you doubted me."

I turn and rush away, shoving through the crowd.

"Jess!"

I push harder, tears blurring my vision as I try desperately to get to an entrance. I find one, but it leads me to a back car lot, very similar to the one Livvie lured me to. I have a brief moment where I know I'm probably being irrational, but it hurts. We'd shared something so beautiful before it.

Something I thought had meant something.

I press myself to a brick wall and I sob, wrapping my arms around myself. I hear the door slam and a moment later Dimitri is in front of me, reaching out.

"Don't touch me," I snarl, shoving his hand away.

"I fucked up. I know you're mad but I wasn't thinking. I regret it, Jess. I didn't question her; instead, I believed you would hurt me before she would—"

"You trusted her over me," I cry, shaking. "You didn't even give me the benefit of the doubt in that hard heart of yours. You just assumed I would be so cold . . ."

He looks away, his jaw tight, his fists clenched. "Can you blame me?"

I flinch.

"Excuse me?" I whisper.

He turns back to me. "You went to Hendrix behind my back only a few days before. Yes you stayed after that, yes you gave yourself to me, but you still did it. You still hid it from me. Of course there was an instant reaction—I thought you cared about me enough to keep Hendrix away, but not enough to stay with me. So I did, I assumed you made sure Hendrix was not going to hurt me before leaving me."

I stare up at him in shock.

"Do you know how much it took me to give myself to you?"

He opens his mouth but I cut him off.

"Do you know how hard it was?"

"Jess . . ."

"Dimitri, I have spent years of my life protecting myself. If I was merely trying to save you because I had no more than tepid feelings for you, then I would have never given myself to you. No, I would have just made sure Hendrix backed off, you backed off, and then I would have left. Instead, I gave you my body but more than that, I let you in and I let you see things no one has ever seen. And you didn't even consider that when Livvie told you I'd run. You just assumed the worst and you acted on it."

"I said I fucked up," he growls. "You should understand how fuckin' hard it is for me with the life I've lived. I don't just trust anyone and even when I do, I find it hard to always see the good. I made a mistake, I don't deny it, but it was an automatic reaction to assume you had betrayed me instead of assuming

Livvie had. Because everyone I've loved in the past has done just that."

I swallow and tears trickle down my cheeks. "The problem with the people you've loved in the past, Dimitri, is that they've loved themselves more than you. In my case, it was very different. I love you more than I've ever loved myself or anything in my life."

He flinches. "What did you say?" he rasps.

"I said I love you, more than life itself."

Suddenly his lips are crushed against mine, his hands are in my hair and he's kissing me with such force that it takes me a second to be able to respond. But when I do, it's explosive. My hands tangle in his hair and I'm kissing him with everything I am, sliding my tongue against his, pressing my body to his, giving him everything. Every ounce of me.

"I fuckin' love you too," he murmurs, before reaching down and taking my legs.

He lifts me up and presses me back against the wall. His hand slides down between us and he shoves my panties aside. I'm thankful in this moment that I'm in a dress. He reaches down and shoves his jeans down, freeing his cock. My entire body comes alive. This is so naughty, so bad, so fucking perfect. There's no foreplay, he's just going to fuck me against this wall, brutal and raw, and it's exactly how I need it.

He takes his cock in his hand and then he's inside me, deep.

I tilt my head back as he starts thrusting into me with pure, male force. He's grunting, I'm moaning his name and our bodies are quickly becoming slick with sweat. His arms bulge as he holds me up while thrusting in and out. His mouth is angry and hungry, nipping and biting my neck. I press my fingers into his biceps and I run my nails down his skin as he fucks me.

Then I come.

It happens quickly and explosively. I scream his name and I feel my entire body wind up tight before I begin pulsing around him, over and over, sending my body into a frenzy. He roars his release only seconds later, using my ass to drive his thrusts, milking himself into my pussy, taking everything, giving everything.

"Fuck, fuck, fuck," he murmurs against my ear.

"I was going to say something similar," I whisper, kissing his earlobe.

"I'm sorry, baby," he says, and I feel a puff of air tickle my neck.

"Don't ever doubt me again, Dimi. I'd never hurt you like that."

He nods and slowly pulls out of me, sliding my panties across. He lets me down gently and pulls his jeans up. He reaches up, running his fingers through my hair while pinning me with his gaze and then he leans in, brushing his lips across mine in a tender kiss that makes me see exactly why he's become my everything.

"Tell me it's finally time to dance?" he rasps.

I smile, big and eager.

"It's finally time to dance."

EPILOGUE

Six Months Later

"Oh God, I feel like a whale!" Indi says, rubbing her very small, rounding belly.

She found out she was pregnant just after they saved me from Roger. They're both thrilled, but so far she's not enjoying growing fatter and fatter each day. I smile and rub her belly too, a little envious. Dimi and I haven't been together long enough to have a baby, but we've sure made a fun time practicing.

"You look beautiful," I assure her.

"Says she," she mutters. "You're making me look like a flea compared to you. When did you get so damned pretty?"

I laugh and shake my head. "You're crazy."

"There you two are."

We turn and see Dimitri and Hendrix coming out with a tray full of steak. We're having a cookout to celebrate my birthday. I beam at the two men, so happy to see they're getting along better. It's not perfect, not by a long shot, but they can have a normal conversation now without wanting to rip each other's head off.

"Did you find Livvie yet, Hendrix?" I ask, standing and making my way over to the two men.

Hendrix shakes his head. "She's good at hiding, but we'll find her."

"And then you'll let me kick her ass."

He laughs. "Absolutely, Jess. She's all yours when we get our hands on her."

I flash him a smile, then step over taking the tray from Dimi's hands. He grins down at me, pressing a kiss to my nose.

"So fuckin' sweet in that dress, Jessie."

I roll my eyes. He adopted the nickname after he heard Hendrix saying it.

"Stop calling me that, it feels . . . dirty somehow."

His grin widens. "I could make it dirty."

I blink innocently at him. "However do you mean?"

His smile grows lazy and he lets his gaze travel down my body.

"Fuckin' womanly things, I'm so hard for you."

I've had my period for the last week, and so poor Dimi has suffered.

"Oh, did I forget to tell you?" I say, placing the tray down and taking a few steps back. "It's gone."

His eyes widen and his expression grows hungry. He lunges at me and I drop the tray, squealing and running around the table.

"You better run, baby, because when I get to you, it's goin' to be quick and damned hard."

He flashes me a wicked grin and chases after me. When he catches me, he leans down, throwing me up and over his shoulder. He slaps my ass and I giggle loudly, causing those around us to groan. He walks me over to the table and places me down, positioning himself in between my legs. He bends to stroke my bottom lip; giving me an expression so deep it takes my breath away.

"I'm goin' to take you home later," he rasps. "And show you exactly how much I love that sweet body, but right now, we have company so I'm goin' to kiss you . . . *just because*."

"Just because why?" I breathe.

He leans down, pressing his lips across mine so tenderly it causes shivers to break out over my body. They go right down to my toes. He strokes my hair as he deepens the kiss, taking me with everything he is. He's giving me all of him and a little bit more, and I couldn't be happier. It would seem he's finally giving me all my dreams wrapped up in one big, gorgeous bow.

"Because," he murmurs, kissing a trail up my cheeks. "You're my everything and you changed my world, Jessie. That's enough of a reason to kiss you every day, for the rest of your life."

ACKNOWLEDGEMENTS

There are so many people I'd like to thank for their help in writing this book. The first of those is my amazing beta reader Sali. For being with me every step of the way when writing this and throwing some seriously good pirate jokes at me. You made this real for me.

I'd love to thank the team from Montlake Publishing for giving this book a chance—I dared to do something different and you believed in me. You've been amazing to work with. It's such an honor.

To my loyal and loving fans—of course I couldn't have made it this far without you. Thank you for always reading and always believing.

Most of all, thank you to my beautiful family. For it's pirates that started me on this journey and it's pirates that made my dreams come true. Without all of you, I could have never done any of this. You've all helped make my dreams come true.

ABOUT THE AUTHOR

Popular romance writer Bella Jewel is the author of the MC Sinners series. An Australian native, Bella calls Far North Queensland home. When not writing, she spends time swimming and having fun with her two daughters. She relishes her career as a writer and is constantly thinking of new book ideas.